THE VALLEY OF DEATH

PER JACOBSEN

– STRUNG II –

THE VALLEY OF DEATH

STRUNG II: THE VALLEY OF DEATH

1st edition, 2022
ISBN: 978-87-973294-8-1

Recognition is an important thing ... but sadly it's also something we often forget to give. Therefore, this book is dedicated to **Janni Buchholt**, *who certainly deserves recognition for all the things she does for others.*

part 1

THE RIVERBED

"In the valley, I saw red.

Neath my soles, I carried it home,

tapped around, watched it spread."

— O. E. Geralt, Red, Red, Riverbed.

— PROLOGUE —

There are no other vehicles on the road and not a single other person in sight. Presumably, there won't be any other people within miles. Still, he takes his foot off the accelerator and brings the car to a halt in front of the bridge.

It's the headlights—more specifically what their cones have brought into focus—that make him do it.

The sight is macabre, cruel. But that's not why he stops and stares at it. By now, he's way too hardened for that. Besides, a hanged human being is no rare sight in this new world.

No, what makes Randall Morgan stop the car are the similarities. Because quite a few things about this scene are almost identical to what he saw on the day it all started.

For you, he corrects himself in his thoughts. *For everyone else, it started two weeks earlier, remember?*

That day he had also stopped because the car's headlights had revealed a hanged man—and back then he *had* been frightened. Because that was the first victim he encountered of the police force's ruthless massacre.

Just as he's alone now, he was also alone in his car on that day. Alone he sat and listened to the eerie scraping of the windshield wipers while he waited for the police to arrive.

The same scraping sound also makes the soundtrack now, although at this moment it's snow and not rain that the rubber strips are pushing aside out on the other side of the windshield glass.

In reality, the resemblance may not be so overwhelming, he thinks, as the wind picks up and turns the lifeless man around. For the dead man he saw back then was blueish-purple and swollen, while the body hanging in front of the vehicle now is practically nothing more than a dried-out skeleton.

But at the end of the day, the biggest change is probably found on his own side of the car's windshield. The man behind the wheel now is not the same as he was then. Much has changed dramatically since the day the world collapsed, and Randall Morgan is by no means an exception.

Before that day, he was a semi-famous writer and part-time father, but from the moment the police officer, one he himself had called for, knocked on the side window and signaled for him to roll it down, everything changed.

From that moment on, he was reduced to prey. A survivor, fleeing from an invisible enemy. An enemy that had the power to get those who had sworn to protect their fellow human beings to kill them instead.

But that role is also a thing of the past. Because Randall is not prey anymore. He's a hunter, chasing one particular person: the traitor who deceived them all. The one who planned the massacre at Redwater football stadium. The leader of the invisible enemy's *new* army.

Randall has to use those kinds of designations when thinking of him now. Otherwise, it hurts too much.

It squeaks and creaks loudly around him as he

puts the car into gear and starts driving. Hopefully, it's just the snow under the tires—and not the steel wires keeping the bridge's carriageway floating—that creates that sound. But it's hard to determine, and he can't be completely sure. Because in a world where nothing is maintained anymore, rust is an ever-growing problem. And the Haywood Bridge wasn't in overwhelmingly good condition to begin with.

The empty streets he drives through are almost without exception covered in a thin layer of snow in which the light of the afternoon sun reflects. The small part of it that succeeds in getting through the gray clouds, that is.

On both sides of the road, he is surrounded by tall buildings, which at the same time seem familiar and alien to him.

Familiar because Randall has been here many times before. Alien, because it was a long time ago—and because nothing looks the way it once did.

The city is Newcrest, and it is—like all other major cities after the Collapse—completely devoid of life.

For what feels like an eternity ago, Randall drove these streets every other weekend, even though he himself lived half a day's journey away. He had to, as this is where his ex-wife moved after the divorce—and she took their son, Billy, with her.

Once, this thought would have filled him with both outrage and sadness, but now it seems ridiculous to him that such small problems could bother him in the past. Besides, it would be pretty futile to stay angry with Allie now, as she most likely isn't alive anymore. She was among those who were infected in the first round and turned into a vegetable when the invasion started.

One of the ones they called *the blanks*.

The blanks are all but gone now. They gradually degraded, both mentally and physically, until at some point they just disappeared. To where, none of the survivors know—just as they can't know for certain that what happened was actually an invasion. But the signs were there. Besides, what other possibility was there? What else could explain how perfectly normal police officers transformed overnight into psychotic murderers who killed innocent people by hanging them from lampposts?

And if not some alien parasite or disease, what could cause almost everyone else to be reduced to empty, mindless shells?

While sitting there behind the wheel, thinking these very thoughts for God only knows which time, Randall picks up a motion out of the corner of his eye: something grayish-brown shooting across the snowy side street on the right side of his car.

He turns his head and feels an intense pain in his abdomen as his brain detects—and then tells his stomach—what it is he has spotted.

A deer. Skinny, but still big enough to keep him—and David, when he comes back—going for at least a week.

Maybe even two, if the temperature doesn't rise too much, he thinks while looking over at the glove compartment where he stores his handgun.

It's tempting, but even though he was trained by his brother during the first few months after the Collapse, Randall still isn't the world's best shooter, so getting the animal would take time. Time that he can't necessarily afford to waste.

He casts one last, wistful glance at the deer, which now leaps over some shallow shrubbery and disappears between two apartment blocks. Then he utters a strained sigh and drives on.

Ten minutes later, he arrives at his destination—and reseeing the place has a strong emotional impact on him. He feels a sting of panic that for a moment paralyzes him and keeps his gaze fixed on the three giant letters on the building's facade.

N.M.H.

NEWCREST MEMORIAL HOSPITAL.

His fingers squeeze so hard around the steering wheel that the knuckles turn as white as the snow covering the asphalt in the large parking lot, and he must concentrate to loosen them and let go.

Once, he set foot here before. That's all. Once, about ... what? A year and a half ago? Two years? Something like that.

He's been to other hospitals since then, in search of the same thing, but not here. Not at Newcrest Memorial Hospital. Because this is where he saw for the first time what their invisible enemy had done to the children.

And this is where he had found his son.

Halfway unconscious and trapped in a trance-like state, Billy had sat among hundreds of other kidnapped children in a dark auditorium within these walls, while some small, disgusting creatures were pumped into their veins. Creatures that probably ...

You need to stop, he thinks, shaking his head from side to side, as if he's literally trying to toss the unwanted images out of his head. *Otherwise, you won't be able to do what you came here for.*

To the right of the hospital entrance, a long roof is mounted on the wall to provide shelter for two-wheeled vehicles. The sight of it—and not least the large hole in one of the roof's tin plates—also brings back memories.

Right now, it's covered in snow, so the strange, missile-like object can't be seen, but he knows it's under there, halfway buried in the asphalt. He also knows he won't gain any useful knowledge by scraping off the snow and studying it. Other—and far smarter—people than him have tried that already.

In fact, it was one of the first things set in motion when the first groups of survivors started to organize after the Collapse. Back then, the desire to understand what had almost wiped mankind off the face of the Earth in two weeks was one of their main driving forces. And so, these objects, which were found scattered in random places across different cities, were studied.

But if those studies have led to anything useful, it's certainly a well-kept secret. Therefore, Randall only offers the snow-covered object a fleeting glance while getting out of the car and walking toward the hospital entrance.

Over there, however, he does slow down and take the time to study the beat-up and burned car, which is lying on its roof—and furthermore is clamped in between the walls on both sides of the entrance. Right in the spot where the entry doors should have been.

The car is a Chevrolet. Once it belonged to Randall's older brother.

The thought of Tommy is allowed to rumble in the back of his head, but only for a second. That's all he can give it. Because thinking of Tommy now is like bursting open a dam in his mind, releasing a flood of shame and guilt.

Shame that he was fooled—and guilt from the responsibility he carries because he didn't see the signs before it was too late.

If only he'd thought it through—*really* thought it through—when he discovered that damned bag in Tommy's backpack, maybe he could have prevented it all. Maybe he could have even stopped the monster who dressed in human skin and hid right under their noses while it planned and set its trap for them.

If only. Those are the words resonating in his mind as he pulls off his thick scarf and wraps it around his hand, so he doesn't cut himself as he leans against the sill and jumps in through the broken window into the hospital entrance hall.

On the other side, he steers directly over to a double door, which leads out to a covered passageway and from there over to an outdoor pavilion.

When he reaches the pavilion, he hesitates for a moment, letting his gaze slide over the doors of the building on the other side until he has located the right one.

In front of the door lies a pile of snow, which he scrapes away with his foot before closing his frozen fingers around the handle.

He pulls. The door doesn't move an inch. For a moment he thinks it's locked, but then he sees the glittering layer that lies across its frame and hinges.

He breathes on his hands, rubs them against each other, and then grabs the door handle once more. Then he pulls.

The ice layer squeaks and then suddenly crumbles in a flurry of small flakes as the door gives way and opens.

He steps into a semi-dark corridor, looks for the staircase that he knows is there, and walks to it.

The lack of electric light darkens the entire building, and he makes sure to hold on to the stair railing so he doesn't fall while he traverses the steps and moves upwards.

What he's looking for is up on the fourth floor.

The hall is on the fourth floor.

Upon opening the door with the large, blue four printed on it and stepping out into the long main corridor, he once again feels the panic stirring.

It is the sight of the sign—and the memories that it brings forth—that causes it.

AUDITORIUM. It's just a word, but it makes his hands quiver and his pulse approach double pace.

Tommy was the first to open the door to the dark hall when they were here last, and for a split second Randall's inner eye reminds him what his brother looked like when he came staggering back from there.

How pale he was. How *terrified* he was.

Randall would probably be greeted by something similar if he stood in front of a mirror now. But it's no use. This has to be done.

With that thought as a driving force, he puts his hand on the handle and pushes the door open. Then, without hesitation, he starts to walk down the long aisle separating the two sections of the auditorium's seat rows.

The same seat rows that last time were occupied by children so pale that they resembled wax figures, and who were unable to do anything but stare blankly up at a screen while their bloodstreams were getting infected with a silvery liquid via a series of IV racks behind the seats.

The children aren't here anymore, but that's no surprise to him. Partly because of what he saw in Redwater, but also because it was the same in the other hospitals. The IV poles and the empty bags on them testified that they had been there, but the children themselves had disappeared.

About halfway down the aisle, Randall slows down and then walks in between the rows of seats on the left side.

It was somewhere around here that they found Billy. He's pretty sure of that. The only problem is that the semi-darkness of the auditorium makes it difficult to navigate, so he has to lean down—almost to the point where he's crawling—to be able to look properly at the floor under the seats.

After a couple of long seconds, during which his gaze glides around down there without spotting anything useful, it starts to feel like a hopeless task. Like it's all been in vain.

Then he sees it; a small, transparent plastic bag lying in the shade from one of the metal posts bolted to the floor to hold the seat rows in place.

His heart beats against his ribs like a trapped animal fighting wildly to escape its cage as he reaches out his hand, grabs the bag, and lifts it up.

In the narrow beam of light slipping in from the door he left open behind him, he looks at the bag, turns it, blinks, looks again ... and feels a relief so strong that it almost brings him to his knees.

Not only does this bag contain almost a quarter of a liter of the silvery liquid that the IV bags in all the other hospitals had been emptied of. There's also at least one of those disgusting tadpole-like creatures left in there.

He can feel it when he presses the bag. A little lump slipping between his fingers.

Dead a long time ago, of course. Nevertheless, it's a specimen that can be studied to hopefully give the remaining survivors more knowledge about their enemy.

It's fragile, perhaps *too* fragile, but this bag—which was once connected to his son's circulation via a thin plastic hose—nevertheless represents a hope.

A hope for the survivors that all isn't lost and that they can perhaps get a step ahead of an enemy who, despite having worn several different masks, has yet to show its true face.

And—for Randall himself—a more modest hope that he will be able to make some kind of sense of what happened at Redwater football stadium. That he will find some understanding of the evil that transformed his personal family tragedy into a tragedy for all mankind, so he can grab it by its roots and tear it up.

And holding such a strong hope in his hands brings the tears out.

THREE MONTHS EARLIER

chapter 1

The sound of the bell didn't reach Randall's consciousness right away. Instead, it snuck in and became part of the nightmare that caused him to twist and turn uneasily in bed that night. And most other nights.

The nightmares were rarely identical, but there seemed to be two elements his subconscious always made sure to reserve a spot for.

One was the auditorium at Newcrest Memorial Hospital, where he had found Billy and the other kidnapped children. The second was the police officer; the huge man who had hurled Randall back and forth over the rain-soaked asphalt on Highway 55, only to try to and hang him from a lamppost afterward.

Actually, it was this very last scene that was

playing out in Randall's subconscious when the high-pitched tones of the bell crept into the dream. They accompanied the raindrops whipping down on him. Added a metallic echo to the soundtrack every time one of the icy drops hit his hands and cheeks as he lay on the asphalt staring up at the officer while he pulled the rope out of the patrol car's trunk.

But while the persistent ringing of the bell was eerie, it was also what ultimately pulled Randall out of the nightmare. Because at some point he registered that something didn't add up. That there was something off—something *asynchronous*—between the rhythm of the bell and the intervals at which the raindrops hit the asphalt. And that discovery shook his consciousness awake, led it to the realization of what bell it was he heard.

That it was Billy's panic bell.

Disoriented, dizzy—and still with the high-pitched tones of the bell resounding in the background—Randall reached out a hand in the dark and let his finger crawl over the wire to the bedside light until he found the switch.

Click. A sea of white light, which felt like acid in his eyes, washed over him.

He forced his legs out over the side of the bed and sat up, rubbing his eyes with one hand.

"You don't need to keep ringing, Billy," he yelled. "I'm on my way."

The bell kept on, undeterred. If anything, it got a little louder.

"Oh, for fuck's sake," Randall growled, but he wasn't really angry, just tired. Besides, even now, at shit-o'clock in the morning, he didn't doubt that giving Billy the bell had been a smart decision. For though the boy had gotten somewhat better over the last thirteen months, he was still dependent on his wheelchair, and he didn't always have sufficient control of his body to be able to speak.

Sometimes, sure. On good days, he could control his vocal cords enough to say—in basic words—if there was anything he wanted or needed help with.

But there were all the other days to consider, too. The ones where he relapsed and seemed more like the empty shell of a human being that they had found in the auditorium at Newcrest Memorial Hospital.

And on those days, the panic bell was a blessing.

And the nights, Randall thought, sighing heavily as he drove his foot into one and then the other slipper. *Don't forget the nights.*

Actually, it wasn't his own voice that presented these two thoughts in his head, but rather a slightly distorted version of his ex-wife's voice. It had been an unwanted side effect of the divorce that Allie had begun to interfere with his thoughts. Especially in situations where his self-esteem was on the lower end.

In time, however, he had gotten so used to it he rarely registered when she popped up to flaunt her opinion.

He left the room and went out into the narrow hallway. It was pitch black, but as it wasn't exactly the first time he had taken this trip at night, he didn't bother to turn on the lights. Instead, he let his fingertips slide over the wallpaper as he walked, until they met the wooden frame, telling him he was at Billy's door.

He found the handle, pressed it down, and gently pushed the door open with his shoulder.

The noisy clatter from the bell stopped almost immediately as the door slid open. However, this didn't mean that the room fell quiet, for the soundscape still contained the boy's jagged, wheezing breath.

It had been one of the bad ones. You didn't need an especially well-developed father instinct to see that.

The boy sat in his bed, rocking from side to side, and even in the sparse lighting—a dusty, bluish beam of moonlight from the window—you could see that he was pale.

Whatever had ripped him out of his sleep had been unpleasant.

"Hey there, BumbleBilly," Randall whispered as he walked to the boy's bedside and sat down next to him. "Daddy's here now. You don't have to be afraid anymore."

No answer—but Randall thought he noticed a slight shift in the boy's breathing. That it got a little calmer. On the other hand, it could have just been something he imagined.

"Did you have a bad dream?"

The answer came—not in words, but in the form of a small, discreet movement in the boy's back. As if a chill ran down it at the memory of the night's experiences.

Randall felt a similar sensation, but immediately suppressed it. He couldn't afford to let these kinds of things set root in him. Then it wouldn't take long before he no longer was able to carry out his most important task. He had to be strong for his son—and that meant that some things simply couldn't be allowed to get under his skin. Otherwise, he could worry himself to death.

With that thought in his head, he snuck the bell out of his son's hand and put it on the bedside table. He then placed his hand on Billy's shoulder and caressed it. This time he wasn't in doubt: the boy calmed down.

A creaking sound made him look over toward the doorway. In it stood the only one of the house's four occupants who didn't bear the last name Morgan.

However, this minor detail didn't mean that David wasn't considered a full member of the family. Because he was. Ever since the day when Tommy and Randall had rescued him from the two officers who assaulted him at the gas station in Ridgeview, David had been a part of their group. He had stuck with them through all the madness, and he had certainly earned the right to call Tommy's farm his home.

"Another nightmare?"

Randall shrugged and nodded.

"It's unbelievable how it just keeps on."

Randall nodded once more—though deep down he didn't find it so unbelievable. Not when you considered how scary it had been inside that auditorium.

"Do you want me to get him some water?"

"Nah, I don't think it's necessary," Randall whispered, looking down at Billy out of the corner of his eye. "I think he's about to fall back asleep."

David gave him a thumbs-up and nodded. Then he began to turn around as if he were going out the door again. Apparently, though, something changed his mind, and instead he snuck over and sat down on a beanbag on the floor on the right side of Billy's room.

"I've got this," Randall whispered. "You don't need to stay."

"It's okay. I'm pretty awake now anyway."

Although these two short sentences were all David said, something told Randall the young man had more on his mind. That there was something he wanted to talk about.

His suspicion apparently was correct, because when Billy finally fell asleep, after sliding gradually down his father's arm and then onto the pillow, David cleared his throat and said:

"If you're not too tired, there's something I'd like to talk to you about. Something I've postponed a couple of times now."

In the wake of both his own and his son's nightmare, Randall was indeed tired, *damned* tired. But he was awake enough to capture the gravity—and something resembling shame—in David's voice. And he didn't have the heart to have the young man put off again what was clearly something he had been building up the courage to talk about.

Thus, Randall simply smiled and waved him to come along.

"We can sit in the kitchen. I was planning on a cup of coffee anyway."

As the weather was warm for the season and the light from the moon played on the leaves of the corn plants out in the field, making it resemble the surface of a quiet, silvery sea, they ended up sitting on the back porch with a couple of blankets.

"So, let's hear it," Randall began, blowing on his coffee and leaning back on the wooden bench. "What is so exciting that it has to be discussed at four o'clock at night?"

"It's about Rose. Or rather ... about me and Rose."

"You're not having problems, are you? I thought you guys were doing so well."

"No, no, it's not that at all," David quickly said. "On the contrary. We're good."

He hesitated for a moment with his eyes looking down at his folded hands and then added:

"Very good, actually."

Suddenly, Randall understood where the conversation was headed and why it was difficult for David.

"That's good to hear," he said. "I'm glad. But you two have also been together quite some time now, haven't you?"

"A year," David said, nodding thoughtfully. "Anniversary next week."

Randall raised one eyebrow and let out a faint whistle. It made David smile and nod.

"Yep, it's pretty crazy. We only just realized it last week, and actually that's the real reason why we ... um, we started talking about maybe ..."

"You're thinking of moving in together," Randall concluded, seeing no reason to prolong the agony. "Is that it?"

David looked to the ground, embarrassed, then nodded again.

"I don't really know why I haven't told you before. Maybe I was a little nervous."

"And for no reason," Randall said, patting him on the shoulder.

His first impulse had been to ruffle the young

man's blond hair, but he managed to stop himself. David wasn't exactly the same, terrified teenager anymore. In many ways, he had become a man over the last year.

"This is fantastic news, David. I'm happy for you guys."

David smiled. Still seemed a little tense, though.

"And if you're worried about the space, don't be," Randall continued. "You'll take my room, of course. It's a little bigger than yours. And if you need more, I'm sure Tommy wouldn't mind us giving the garage workshop a little makeover. His Harley Davidson is just standing there anyway, and he hardly ever touches it. Out there, you'd have plenty of space."

"Oh yeah, that sure does sound cool, but we ... kind of figured that I'd be moving in with her."

"Oh, okay. Sure, that's ... that makes perfect sense, too. I mean, their group has plenty of space."

"Yeah ... yeah, exactly."

After those words followed a pause. A *long* pause. Then Randall cleared his throat.

"What about Tommy? Did you tell him?"

"Yeah, well, yes and no. He knows, but I didn't tell him. Dylan overheard me and Rose talking about it a few days ago. He promised me that he wouldn't say anything until we made it official, but then ..."

"But then he played poker with Tommy and the other dorks from the cleanup crew," Randall concluded for him, and David nodded.

"Yeah, we're constantly discovering new stuff that we're missing since the Collapse, but the booze never seems to run out, and neither does its *Best before* date. Sadly."

"You've been over there much more than me. Does he have it under control?"

"Tommy?"

Randall nodded.

"I'm not sure. But I definitely don't think it's gotten easier for him since he joined the cleanup crew, hanging out with Jack and the others."

"You can say that again," Randall sighed. "He spends more and more time over there. You have to promise me that you'll keep an eye on him."

"Perhaps you should consider tagging along

when I move? I mean, there's space and resources for both you and Billy. It might even be good for him to have more people around. Takes a village and all that. And you know they're crazy about him over there. The child who survived. The miracle boy."

Out in the field, the wind took hold of the corn plants and pulled them from side to side, so the quiet, silvery surface momentarily was turned into a rough sea.

"Not everyone," Randall said. "Many in San Hiva see it as a miracle that Billy survived, yes. But *not* all of them."

"I know some of them are worried that he might be ... *dangerous* with the whole hospital thing. But seriously, so were we. In the beginning, I mean. As soon as they get to know him, they'll see that he wouldn't harm a fly."

Randall stared blankly up at the night sky for a moment, then shook his head.

"Nah, it's a bad idea. Billy needs routine. Familiarity. And he knows the farm. From both before and after it all went to hell. I'm not sure he could handle a completely new environment."

"Maybe you could try it for a while, just to see if—"

"But I'm happy for you, David. Really. When do you plan on moving out?"

"Uh, okay. I ... I plan to spend the rest of the week packing my stuff. I don't have *that* much, but it'll still be a bunch of boxes. And then I guess the move could be done over the weekend."

"So, in three or four days?"

David nodded, and Randall took a sip of his coffee, hoping it would seem as if that was what made him grimace and make a strained swallowing motion.

For although he had been telling the truth when he said he was happy for David, the news was still a bit of a blow to the stomach.

What did you expect? That you would live on the farm forever, cut off from the outside world like the lost boys on Neverland?

"Sounds reasonable," he said. "And you can count on us to give you a hand, of course."

"Thanks. In any case, I'm definitely going to

need Tommy's truck for all my junk."

"Mm, let's just hope it isn't gonna rain."

"Yeah, stuff like this was a little easier back when we had weather forecasts."

Randall nodded but said nothing. He simply emptied his coffee cup and proceeded to stare out over the field while thinking about how spot-on David was.

Because yes, things were easier before, when you were warned in advance that the wind was gonna change and there might be a storm brewing.

chapter 2

When the day of David's move arrived, both Randall and David were up before the sun. And when it drew its first delicate pink brushstrokes over the clouds in the distance, they were almost done loading the cardboard boxes aboard Tommy's truck.

The driver himself, however, was nowhere to be seen. He didn't get up until a few hours later when the smell of eggs and bacon reached his room.

"Oh, so you decided to get out of bed and join the party?" were the words Randall chose to greet his older brother with as Tommy stepped into the kitchen. He could easily have found a snider alternative—and truth be told, it would only have been fair to do so—but the mood was tense enough with the move and all.

"Morning," Tommy muttered, pulling a chair

out from under the table. "The alarm didn't ring. How far along are you?"

"We're almost done."

"Christ. Why didn't you wake me up?"

"Shouldn't be necessary. You're a grown man. Besides, I didn't think you'd be worth much if you didn't get some sleep. You came home pretty late last night."

"That's exactly right, Randall," Tommy sneered. "I *am* a grown man. So maybe it's none of your business at all what time I get home."

"The eggs are a little cold, but if you grab a plate, I can heat a portion for you, Tommy."

The bright, melodic voice that joined the conversation, thereby interrupting a burgeoning argument between the two brothers, belonged to Rose. She had spent the night at the farm so she could help with the move.

"Thank you, Rose," Tommy said, after which he followed her suggestion and took a plate from the cabinet.

Throughout his life, Randall had only met a few people who could handle Tommy as elegantly as

Rose had just done. She had a knack for disarming him in situations where the rebellious part of his personality was about to take over. And for someone like Tommy, that meant he was saved from a lot of trouble when she was around.

"I'm thinking we'll drive in two cars," Randall said after Tommy had taken a seat at the table. "Me, Rose, and Billy will take the Ford, while David and you take the truck with all the boxes. Then we can stay ahead and warn you if we come across any patrols. You will have to drive extra slowly today with the load."

Tommy stared at him while dumping a small, triangular piece of fried egg in his mouth and chewing it slowly.

"There *won't* be any patrol cars."

"I know we haven't seen any in a while," Randall replied. "But still, it doesn't hurt to be careful."

"Of course it doesn't," Rose added, brushing one of Tommy's long, gray hairs off his shoulder. "Tommy knows that, too. How are the eggs?"

"Yum," Tommy said, giving her a thumbs-up.

Rose replied with a smile and then walked over

to her seat next to Billy and David.

At this side of the table, her cheerful nature also rubbed off on the others. David took her hand and gave it a loving squeeze, while Billy began rocking back and forth in his wheelchair with a smile on his lips.

"Have you had anything to eat yourself, babe?"

Rose put her hand on her stomach and stroked it as if she wanted to make sure before answering David's question. Then she wrinkled her nose and shook her head.

"No thank you. I was a bit nauseous this morning, and I'm not very hungry."

Rose was a charming girl. You couldn't take that away from her. And it wasn't hard to understand what David saw in her. Nevertheless, it hurt Randall a bit that the young man was in such a hurry to move in with her.

Part of it was because of Billy. After all, David was one of the three people closest to him, and it could be hard for the boy when he suddenly wasn't there every day.

The second part of it was more selfish. Over the

past year or so, Randall had begun to consider David a close family member, almost like a son, and this of course meant it was hard that he had now decided to leave the nest.

Especially since the world he was up against wasn't very forgiving. Tommy might be right in that there had been a thinning-out of the patrols (meaning the number of brainwashed, murderous policemen hanging innocent people up in lampposts) but that didn't change the fact that the new world was harsh. Resources were constantly getting sparser, and there weren't many technological aids left either.

"Then just a quick trip to the crapper to move my bowels, and I'll be ready to move the other stuff," Tommy muttered as he chewed the last forkful he had just thrown in his mouth.

"Charming, as ever," Randall said, shaking his head. Then he turned to David. "What do you say we get the boxes strapped to the back of the truck while he handles that... project?"

David looked down at his plate and then up at Rose, who nodded.

"Go ahead. I'll handle the dishes."

"You're an angel, Rose," Randall said. "Should we say the driveway in ten minutes?"

Rose looked down at the plates on the dining table and then over at the kitchen sink.

"Let's make it fifteen."

With those words, the agreement was made, and fifteen minutes later all five of them met outside. There they split up into the two cars and started driving down the long dirt road that connected the driveway of Tommy's remote farm with East Alin's larger access roads.

The first half-hour of the drive was quite undramatic. Of course, many of the things they passed would have been deeply disturbing to a viewer who hadn't lived through the attack from their invisible enemy and witnessed the fall of the orderly world.

But the five people in the two cars had indeed experienced it. So shocking them would take more than the empty streets, the overgrown gardens, and the corpses, which were so dissolved and rotten that they could barely keep themselves hanging from the lampposts and signs to which they were tied.

In fact, East Alin wasn't so bad anymore. On the one hand, the clean-up crews, like the one Tommy was a part of, had removed many of the hanged, and on the other hand, the bodies had stopped smelling over time. As a general rule. Every now and then you could still stumble upon a *real stinker*, as Tommy used to call them.

While sitting there in the driver's seat watching the lifeless streets of what had once been *his* city, it was such thoughts that occupied Randall's mind. And he was so engrossed in them that he jolted when Rose's hand shot forward from the back seat and touched his shoulder.

"Slow down a bit," she said. "I'm not entirely sure, but I think I saw something."

Randall turned around in the seat and met her gaze. Told her, without words, to elaborate.

"I'm not sure," she repeated. "But I caught something out of the corner of my eye just now. Something that could have been a car."

"Where?"

"Behind the fence over by the construction site.

Something whizzed by on the other side of it."

"Color?"

Before answering, Rose hesitated long enough for Randall to already know the answer. Still, he swallowed a lump when she bit her lower lip and said:

"Well, it *was* white ... but I don't know if it was a police car."

"Shit. You couldn't tell if it had a crest on the door, could you?"

Rose shook her head and gave him an apologetic look.

Randall nodded, raised one hand from the steering wheel, hesitated for a moment, and then reached for the walkie they had installed in the car.

"Tommy?" he said after pressing the button.

For a few seconds, a faint, metallic hum was the only sound. Then there was a click, followed by David's voice.

"No, it's me, David. Tommy's got the wheel. Is something wrong?"

"It's probably nothing," Randall replied, glancing back at Rose, who approved the interpretation with a slight nod. "But Rose thinks she saw a car drive by behind the construction site next to Hillmoore. A white car, mind you."

"Okay ... But not a patrol car, right?"

"We're not sure, but in any case, it's probably a good idea to be a little extra careful from now on."

"Of course. Was it headed in the same direction as us? Did she ... Did you see that, Rose?"

Randall looked to the back seat, where Rose was adjusting Billy's cap, which had slid down over his eyes. She met his gaze and shrugged.

"I think it drove parallel to us," she said. "But I only saw it for a short second out of the corner of my eye, so I could easily be wrong."

"Did you get that, David?"

"Yeah, we heard."

"Good, and what are you thinking? Should we hold the course or find another way?"

"Just a sec."

Another short click from the walkie's speaker told them that David had disconnected.

While they waited for him to return, Randall slowed down a bit more. The needle of the gauge was now dancing around forty miles per hour.

The slower speed gave him time to study the surroundings outside the car more thoroughly than he would normally have done. He saw new details he hadn't noticed before, which were both scary and impressive at the same time.

One of these was the plants. East Alin may not have been the world's largest town, but that still was the definition: a *town*. Yet it was nature and plant life that had begun to take over. In the time that had passed since the Collapse, the hedges around the gardens of the empty houses had started to overtake the pavements and the edges of the roads. Especially the hedges that were made of climbers.

And where there were holes in the asphalt, there were, almost without exception, also small clusters of dandelions and other weeds to spot.

Life finds a way, popped up in the back of his head, and he knew instinctively it was something he had heard in a movie. He just couldn't remember which one.

He never found the answer, because now he

caught sight of Tommy's truck in the rearview mirror, and that—combined with another scratchy sound from the walkie's speaker—ripped him out of his stream of thoughts.

"Are you there?"

"We're here, David."

"Okay. Tommy thinks we should just go on. And I kind of agree."

Randall caught Rose's eye in the rearview mirror. She nodded.

"Fair enough. It's your call. But let us know if there's the slightest sign of trouble."

"We will. You too."

After those words, David cut the connection once more, and the car was filled with silence.

Oh, well, if you ignored Billy, who had started making a hissing sound. It almost sounded like he was trying to whistle but couldn't.

By the time they reached the end of Saxton Road and turned left onto Pineview, there had been no sign of the mysterious white car. The same was true when they left Pineview again—and upon reaching the city limits and leaving East Alin a little later,

Randall had almost forgotten all about it.

Right up until it appeared in the rearview mirror far behind them. A blurry white silhouette that was slowly but surely gaining ground on Tommy's truck.

Without shifting his gaze from the rearview mirror, Randall grabbed the walkie's transmitter again.

"David?"

"Yeah, we see it ... and yes, it is a patrol car."

chapter 3

In the seconds after receiving David's confirmation that the white car was a police car, it was no longer Randall's conscious mind that steered the vehicle he, Billy, and Rose were in.

It was instinct. Triggered by the deep-seated fear, which had laid dormant within him since his first encounter with a police officer in the new world, it simply took over. It shut down everything else and forced his one hand to tear the steering wheel hard to the left, while the other pulled the handbrake.

With Rose's shocked scream and the squeals from the tires as a dramatic accompaniment, the old black Ford slid sideways over the asphalt until it had turned to face Tommy's truck. And the white car that had now almost caught up to it.

Here, closer, Randall could see them, too. The cursed crests that had once represented a promise to serve and protect—and had since become a promise to lynch and kill.

"Hold on," he said, without turning around to see if Rose and Billy actually followed that order—and without really knowing what the next step of the plan would be once he had put the pedal to the metal.

But to the metal it went, and the Ford was pulled forward at tremendous speed while he leaned to the side and opened the glove compartment.

From it, he pulled a Smith & Wesson SD9 handgun, which he handed Rose. Then he grabbed the walkie's transmitter and did the same with it.

"Tell them to make a turn at the intersection," he said. "A sharp one. Then we'll make a distraction. See if we can get it to follow us instead."

Rose didn't respond, but when he looked in the rearview mirror, he could see that she had picked up the transmitter and held it in front of her mouth.

"David?" she said in a voice that, given the situation, was astonishingly calm. "David, can you hear me? You need to make a turn at the intersection. Then we'll try to lure it away from you."

A few seconds went by before David answered—and those seconds his girlfriend didn't waste. She checked that the gun was loaded and that the safety was off, after which she moved to the side and rolled down the left rear window.

"We'll take a sharp turn. Got it, Rose," David's voice sounded in the speaker, and after a pause he added—with a tenderness in his voice that made Randall's heart sink: "Be careful, babe."

"I will. You too."

With that, Rose handed the transmitter back to Randall. She then leaned over to the window again and stuck out her arm. Seconds later, her hand—and the gun it was holding—appeared on the edge of Randall's field of view.

There it lingered, astonishingly steady, just outside his window, while the distance between them and the white car, yard by yard, dwindled.

When the truck reached the intersection and Tommy turned sharply to the right, the patrol car continued straight ahead, towards them, just as they had hoped.

But even though that part went according to plan, there was something about the sight of the patrol car as it got closer that didn't feel right to Randall.

Because there were two people in the car, and it looked as if one of them was almost crawling out the window on the passenger side. And even in light of all the crazy things he'd seen police officers do in the new world, this was a bizarre behavior.

What the hell is he doing? he thought, and he was about to say this very thought aloud to Rose, when he picked up a detail of the man that made him stiffen.

The detail was the big red bird from the game *Angry Birds*. It was printed in the middle of the man's dark blue T-shirt.

"Don't shoot, Rose!"

"What? What do you mean?"

"They're not police officers!"

"But ... what? I don't understand ..."

"Look at his T-shirt."

Rose said nothing, but the gun stayed outside

Randall's window long enough to make him fear that she would fire it despite the new information. But she ended up lowering it, and the bang that otherwise would probably have shattered his eardrum never came.

There was, however, another sound that found its way to his ear canal, now that the patrol car had come even closer. And should there still have been a flicker of doubt in his mind, that sound settled the matter.

It *wasn't* policemen in that vehicle. Hell, they were barely *men*.

"What a couple of idiots," Rose said, as the sound—a long wolf howl from the young man hanging and waving his arms halfway out of the patrol car's side window—also reached her. "You'd almost hope they would crash."

Hardly had she finished the sentence before she threw her hand up to her mouth and looked shamefully over at Billy and then at Randall.

"Oh God, I'm sorry," she said. "I was just scared. I didn't mean—"

"Idiooots," Billy repeated from the other side of

the back seat.

Maybe it was the nerves and the shock following the experience. Maybe it was because it was the first real word the boy had said today ... or perhaps it was because he delivered it with a twinkle in his eye, which he rarely had.

Whatever it was, it made both Rose and Randall break out in laughter. Not the roaring *HA HA*-kind, but rather the kind where the stomach pulls together involuntarily, and small bursts of gurgling coughs shoot up through the throat, whether you try to hold them back or not. And it didn't get any better when Billy realized it was his comment that had them laughing and decided to join the chorus.

Now they sat there like three dumb cats trying to cough up hairballs. And why? Because a couple of punks had somehow gotten their hands on a police car and were now hanging out of its window while driving around, trying to scare the crap out of people.

That was one interpretation as to why they were laughing. Another was that for a moment they had thought they were actually being chased by real police officers. That they were going to die.

This thought became the valve cap needed to shut off Randall's hysterical chuckling. And while the other two also quietly regained control over their bodies, he grabbed the walkie's transmitter.

"David, do you read me?" he said. "It was a false alarm."

David must have been ready with his walkie in his hand because the answer came immediately:

"False alarm? What's that supposed to mean?"

"It was a police car, but it wasn't officers driving it. It was two young guys ... some *punks*. They must have stolen it or something."

This time it was Tommy's voice that sounded in the speaker.

"That's gotta be some of the stupidest shit I've ever heard," he said. "Even I wouldn't do anything that dumb."

"And that's saying something," Randall replied. "But hey, if they do get caught by a couple of real cops, I'm guessing they'll regret it."

"Oh man, just imagine," said David, who had apparently gotten the transmitter back. "So, what do we do now? Drive back, meet with you at the intersection, and then follow the original plan?"

"Yeah. And then we pray that the rest of the trip will be a little less exciting."

chapter 4

It turned out that the incident involving the two troublemakers in the patrol car was only allowed to retain the spot as the morning's most dramatic event for a very short time.

The time at which it was beaten was 11:27 a.m., and the place was a wooded area east of Gleamsdale. Here, the two cars—Randall's Ford and Tommy's truck—were driving on separate hilltops in a dull, weathered landscape when Randall was ripped out of his thoughts because Billy's bell started ringing in the back seat.

"What's the matter, hon?" he asked, and when that triggered no response from the boy, he added, "Rose, do you mind?"

"On it," sounded from the back seat. "Is it the seat belt, Billy? Is it hurting your neck again?"

Billy's answer came in two parts: First, a sound that was a strange middle ground between a child's wail and a cat's wheeze, then three quick rings with the bell.

A *no* and an *exclamation point* would, in Randall's experience, be the closest translation.

"The window?" Rose continued. "Why are you pointing at the window? Are you cold? Is that it? Is there a draft?"

She began to reach over the boy, but he immediately shook his head and grabbed a cluster of his own light bangs.

"C-caap," he got out after a few unsuccessful attempts.

"Oh, your cap," Rose said, pretending to hit herself on the forehead. Then she looked around; first on the seats, then at the bottom of the car, and finally on the back dash behind them.

"Sorry," she said. "I don't see it anywhere, Billy."

"Caap," Billy repeated. "Cap b-back."

"Well, I'm trying to get you your cap back, but I just can't find it. Did you perhaps—"

"Back, b-back!" Billy insisted, staring at her with

a look that would have been quite offensive if one didn't know about the boy's condition. "Cap. Back. Cap. Back!"

In the mirror, Randall saw Billy finish his speech by turning his face—in a quick jolt—away from Rose, as if deeply offended by her denseness.

Disability or not, this was completely unacceptable behavior by Randall's book, and he was about to inform his son when he realized that Billy might not have turned his face *away* from Rose so much as he had turned it *toward* something else.

"Not *get back*," he said, catching Rose's gaze in the rearview mirror. "We're guessing at the wrong verb. I think he's trying to tell us we need to *go* back."

Billy rang his bell once and slapped his thigh with his other hand.

"But what does that even ..." Rose began, but then the answer apparently came all by itself. "Oh, right. Now I get it. You lost your cap. It went out the window, didn't it?"

Billy put his hands up and shook them as if saying: *Sure took you long enough!*

"Was it just now?"

The boy answered Rose's question with an eager nod, after which he gave an elaborate explanation in the form of a lot of sounds, which unfortunately only made sense to himself. Meanwhile, Randall pulled over and parked the car by the side of the road. Then he once again grabbed the walkie.

"David?"

"You're a couple of chatterboxes today, aren't you?" David replied cheerfully, but almost immediately—perhaps because he remembered the incident with the patrol car—his voice took a more serious tone. "Is something wrong?"

"Nothing too serious," Randall said. "It's just Billy. He dropped his baseball cap out the window."

"The red one?" Tommy interjected in the background.

"Yep. The wind must have pulled it off."

"Oh, damn. That sucks. He loves that one."

Randall had to swallow a lump before continuing. Because his brother was right; Billy loved that cap very much. So much, in fact, that Randall sometimes had a nagging feeling that the boy's feelings for it could easily compete with those he had for the people who surrounded him.

"Yeah ... yeah, he does. Anyway, I just wanted to let you know that we've stopped to look for it, and if you could keep your eyes open as well, just in case it's in the ditch, that would be good."

"Sure. We will."

"Thanks."

After the conversation, Randall put the Ford in reverse and started to roll slowly backward, while he, Rose, and Billy closely studied the landscape around the car.

Moss-covered tree trunks, boulders surrounded by piles of brown leaves, and clusters of forest floor plants so dried up that they looked almost dark gray ... but no bright red cap.

When he had backed almost all the way up to the top of the hill they were on, Randall once again stopped the car. It was, to his best estimate, somewhere around here that Billy had started ringing the bell.

Apparently, Billy agreed, because now he knocked one hand's knuckles against the back window and pointed down towards the slope that began by the roadside.

"It looks steep," Rose said.

That wasn't a lie. The slope *did* look steep, very steep—even if there were a fair amount of trees to lean on. An unfortunate fall there could result in a pretty rough rollercoaster ride.

Randall had that thought. But what he said out loud while he loosened the buckle and got out was:

"It looks worse than it is."

Rose didn't answer, but simply followed his example and got out of the car.

"Should we take the chair out of the trunk?"

"Nah, it's not worth the trouble. He'll have to wait up here anyway, so he might as well stay in the car."

Rose nodded and then shrugged while exchanging a glance with Billy. The boy just smiled and made a *no worries* gesture with his hand.

"Rock, paper, scissors?" Rose asked when they had come all the way out to the edge.

"I'll do it," Randall replied. "You can wait here with Billy."

"What? Because I'm a girl or what?"

Randall didn't answer right away. He needed time to analyze her voice and her facial expressions. Was she actually offended? No, he didn't think so.

"Something like that," he said, smiling as she replied with what his ex-wife would have described as *the scoff of a true princess.*

The steep decline meant he had to move slowly, and Randall hadn't gotten very far before he heard a vehicle pull in and stop behind the Ford up on the road.

Tommy's truck. The bubbling rumble of its engine was unmistakable—and should he have been in doubt still, the matter was settled when the engine sound was replaced by a deafening whistle.

"Hey, wait up!"

Randall slowed down a bit, turned around ... and sighed. Not because Tommy had told him to wait, but because he was hoping to hear something else from his brother's mouth. But apparently, they hadn't had any success in locating the damned cap either.

A new sound—twigs snapping—made him turn around again.

It was Rose. She had snuck past behind his back and was now some way ahead of him.

With her turquoise jacket, her red hair, her pink, freckled cheeks, and her *fooled you, old man* smile, she looked completely out of place in this gray, dried-out forest. As if she were the only colorful part of an otherwise dull painting.

As if she were the only living thing, he thought, and the thought gave him goosebumps, even though he didn't quite know what it meant.

He realized that she was also staring at him—with a look of anticipation.

"Yeah," he said, nodding. "I get it. You're a badass ninja princess that no man can hold back. Fair enough, have it your way. As long as you're careful. I'll go up to Billy, then."

Rose pulled out the bottom edges of an invisible dress and curtsied, after which she turned around and disappeared from view behind some large tree trunks.

He started walking back in the direction of the

road that Tommy and David had just left. They were now moving towards him. Just as he and Rose had done, they went in a zigzag pattern, so they always had a tree to lean on.

A couple of times Tommy was close to losing his footing on the undergrowth and the loose dirt, but David—probably due to his younger age—didn't have the same trouble keeping his balance. However, Randall refrained from taunting Tommy with it like he normally would have. Perhaps because the expression on Tommy's face made it clear that he *wasn't* enjoying himself.

"Where is Rose?" David asked as they met halfway.

Randall pointed down to the spot where Rose had disappeared behind the trees.

"Somewhere down there."

He saw lines of worry crawl across David's face and added:

"Don't worry, she's only a little bit ahead of us. You'll easily catch up with her."

The worried wrinkles in David's forehead lingered for a moment before they disappeared. But even though they were gone, he still picked up the pace to catch up with his girlfriend.

"Goddamnit!" Randall heard a voice say, and as he turned around, he saw his older brother embracing a tree trunk. Clinging to it.

"This is irresponsible and dangerous," Tommy continued. "But not in a fun way."

Randall nodded—and suppressed a smile that was very eager to show itself.

"Yes, I kind of agree that it might be a little *too* risky. I mean, it's a cap. Not exactly worth breaking a leg over."

Tommy caught his eye and raised one eyebrow.

"Except we both know it's not *just* a cap."

Randall took a deep breath and let it out in a long sigh. Then he nodded and continued up the slope.

Seven yards. That was as far as he got before the sound of Rose's voice made him stop. She was yelling from somewhere down among the trees ahead.

First with enthusiasm and the melodic sound that was her trademark. Next, with a confusion and panic that made the nerve threads in Randall's spine feel as if they had been coated in ice.

"IT'S DOWN HERE, I FOUND IT!" was the first thing she shouted.

"NO, WHAT IS ... OH GOD, WHAT *IS* THAT?" was the next.

chapter 5

The baseball cap indeed lay on the forest floor, as eye-catching as a giant red balloon would have been—and with the image of Baby Yoda and the text *DON'T MAKE ME USE THE FORCE* written across the front, there was no doubt that it was Billy's cap.

Yet, none of the four people who had been searching for it bent down and picked it up. In fact, not a single one of them offered it more than a fleeting glance.

Because once they had seen what was behind it, down at the end of the slope, their attention was locked on that.

The dried-out riverbed was squeezed in between a series of gloomy ridges and rocky outcrops. An elongated, crescent-shaped notch in the landscape that, with the right lighting—and under other circumstances—could have been a divine sight. The kind of landscape people would use as a screensaver on their computers and mobile phones.

But as it stood now, there was nothing divine about the valley and the dry riverbed cutting through it. Hell, no gods—at least none of the ones Randall could think of—would willingly have taken credit for this.

Hundreds? Thousands? Randall's brain couldn't even speculate, but what it was able to decipher was that the dead bodies were everywhere, evenly spread out across the entire valley. Except over on the right side, about ten to fifteen yards inside the parched riverbed, where several were stacked in one place. They lay in a pyramid-shaped pile on top of each other.

If one were to let their gaze slide in a straight line upwards from the tip of the pyramid, the explanation was pretty straightforward, however.

Far above the pile, a rocky plateau stuck out, and the pyramid had to be a result of these people either being thrown—or having thrown themselves—

over the edge of it.

"What kind of *sick* shit is this?"

"A mass grave," Randall replied, mostly as an automatic reflex. Deep down, he was well aware, obviously, that the question was rhetorical, and that Tommy was perfectly capable of drawing that conclusion for himself. "Somebody killed a hell of a lot of people."

Again, he was about to add, but then didn't. Partly because he stopped himself, and partly because he was interrupted by an unpleasant sound when Rose fell to her knees and emptied the contents of her stomach on top of a knotty root that stuck up from the ground farther down the slope.

Almost simultaneously, David followed her example, and for a moment Randall was also disturbingly close to giving in to the increasing nausea in his throat. But he was once more interrupted. This time by his ex-wife's voice, invading his thoughts again.

Is this it, Randall? she asked. *Is this how round three begins?*

The question caused his stomach to shrink and

tie a knot around itself. And the answer—*what other explanation could there be?*—which popped up in his head just tightened that knot even more.

"Not somebody," he heard Tommy say behind him. "Them."

"What?"

"You said that *somebody* killed a lot of people," Tommy elaborated. "But it wasn't *somebody*. It was them. They did it themselves."

For a while, Randall stood with his eyes directed at everything and nothing out in the dry riverbed, while the words of his brother slowly started to make sense.

And the longer he spent studying the bodies, the clearer it became to him that Tommy was indeed right: these people didn't appear to have *been* killed. They looked to have taken their own lives.

Some with the guns that were scattered on the ground, some by throwing themselves off the cliff. All of them with the same result.

He narrowed his eyes. There was something else. Another realization, hiding right below the surface, that he just couldn't get a hold of.

Then it came to him: This couldn't be the start of the next round of the invasion, as Allie had suggested in his thoughts.

For death wasn't the only thing that the many people who lay on the ground in the parched riverbed had in common. They also had their uniforms. Some were light brown, some blue, and others black—but all of them were police uniforms.

"Why on Earth would they throw away their strongest weapon?" asked Tommy, who apparently had made the same observation.

Randall had no answer, at least not one he was ready to say out loud, so he just shrugged his shoulders and went over to Rose and David.

They both sat crouched in the places where they had been overpowered by nausea. Rose had tears in her eyes, and the skin on her face had turned so pale it made her freckles look completely black.

Whether her boyfriend was pale, Randall couldn't tell, as David hadn't lifted his head yet. He just sat on all fours staring down at a puddle of his own vomit. Perhaps he was waiting for the thin thread of saliva stretched out between his mouth and the puddle to break by itself so he wouldn't have to touch it.

The thread snapped the very moment when Randall stopped next to David and stretched out his hand.

He accepted it, let himself be pulled up—and when he got on his feet, Randall thought for a moment that David was gonna throw himself into his arms to be embraced and comforted. Because for a moment he didn't look like the young man with whom he had loaded boxes on the truck this morning so he could move in with his girlfriend. For a moment he looked like the other David; the teenager with the hoodie and the frightened look who they had picked up and made part of their group shortly after the Collapse.

In the end, it was the adult version of David that took control: his eyes became small, his face hard, and he walked without hesitation over to Rose, helped her up and held her tight.

"I'm sorry," she said in a quavering voice, as she caught Randall's eye over David's shoulder. "It ... it was just that ... it all came back to me at once, you know."

She didn't explain further and didn't need to. It had taken months before she trusted him and Tommy enough to share her story with them, but in the end, they had gotten it.

And of the many stories Randall had heard about how the psychopathic police force had made the first two weeks following the invasion a living hell for the survivors, Rose's story was possibly the worst.

Because Rose came from Coulton, a small rural town with a population in the very low end, and the two rangers who made up the entire police force out there had been effective. So effective, in fact, that Rose—who was still just a high school student at the time—saw half of all the people she knew get murdered in cold blood over just three days. And the rest were turned into mindless vegetables, so there was no help and no comfort to be found for her anywhere.

An outright massacre, it was. Nothing less.

So yeah, Randall knew what Rose meant when she said it *came back to her*—and it made his heart ache.

"I still don't get it," Tommy said with such pure astonishment in his voice that you'd think it was something he'd spent several years—and not just the last few minutes—trying to find an answer to. "What do they gain from doing this?"

Again, Randall had no answer, but David did.

"Maybe they've just ... reached their expiration date?" he suggested.

Tommy squinted.

"What do you mean?"

David hesitated and let his eyes slide out across all the dead people in the riverbed. Then he nodded to himself.

"We never really talk about it," he said. "Maybe because we don't like the idea. But I think most of us—of the survivors, I mean—would agree that what happened to the officers back then was some kind of ... possession. That something controlled them like ..."

"Like puppets," Rose concluded, and David nodded.

"Exactly. And maybe there was some sort of

expiration date on how long they could do it. How long their bodies could take it, I mean. Or ... nah, I don't know. Maybe it's too far out."

Tommy uttered a nervous snort and bit his lower lip.

"So, you're saying someone flicked a power switch and made all these people shut down all at once? Just like that."

He gave the last word a dramatic underline by snapping his fingers—and it worked. The sharp sound echoed through the valley with an eerie reverberation.

"Either that," David said, nodding, "or they were pre-programmed to turn off now."

A thought—fleeting but unpleasant—entered through the back of Randall's mind. Had something similar happened when the blanks disappeared? Were they also *pre-programmed* to shut down, as David called it? And if so, was Allie, his ex-wife and Billy's mother, lying somewhere out there right now, rotting away in the middle of some pyramid of dead people?

That thought led him to a new question:

"How long have they been here? And how did they even get out here? On foot?"

"Not too long," Tommy replied. "They don't look particularly dried up, and ... the smell isn't too bad either."

Randall nodded, although he wasn't sure whether they were actually able to determine how bad the smell was down here. Most things smelled a bit worse in the new world, and over time you built up a kind of immunity to it.

But no, he guessed that Tommy was probably right; it would have been worse if they had been lying here for a long time.

"But how the hell they got all the way out here..." Tommy said, grabbing his neck. "That beats me."

"I think I have an idea."

It was David—but when Randall and Tommy turned their heads towards him to hear what the idea was, the young man had already turned his back on them and was climbing the slope over on the right side of the valley. The one that led up the side of the plateau.

Halfway up, he paused with one hand resting on

a tree trunk and the other on his forehead, shading his eyes from the sun.

"I was right," he announced in a strange mixture between a shout and a whisper. "Their cars are up there."

He pointed up to the rocky outcrop and then added:

"And there's a lot of them."

Randall was curious, but he was also getting more and more aware that Billy was still sitting in the Ford, so when Tommy with a small hand gesture asked if he was coming, he shook his head.

"I'd better get back to the car. Billy's still up there."

"Do you want me to go with you?" a voice sounded a little further ahead.

"No, it's okay, Rose. Why don't you just go up there with them? I'll see you in a minute."

With those words, Randall went over and picked up Billy's cap from the ground, after which he turned around and looked up the slope with narrowed eyes. Studied it.

It was a long way to the top—and how the cap

had ended up all the way down here was a mystery to him.

In any case, it had to have rolled most of the way, he concluded, as he began to make his way back along the same route that he had followed to get down there.

The hike back was strenuous, and once he had reached the top, he had to take a break to catch his breath—and perhaps also to get a moment to process the shock—before walking the last twenty yards to the car.

That is what he said to himself, a small break before continuing. But when the other three came back, he was still sitting there by the side of the road, staring blankly into the air as he turned Billy's red cap aimlessly back and forth in his hands.

part 2

SAN HIVA

"What truly fascinates me is what happens the day we run out of bullets."

— O. E. Geralt

chapter 6

With a measly total of two streets perpendicular to each other, San Hiva was one of the smallest towns in the entire county, and had it not been for the coal mine, it would have been hard to justify the town's existence in the old world.

Ironically, its modest size was also the factor that made San Hiva one of the most populated cities in the new world. Although that wasn't saying much. The last official population count Randall had heard was sixty-eight.

And with David, that number would be sixty-nine.

Most buildings in San Hiva were made for commerce ... although the majority now looked like empty sets from old western films with their torn, sun-bleached awnings and their dirty facade windows.

People would also be a rare sight for a traveler passing near the traffic light, which hung over the city's only intersection, swaying in the wind. This had two explanations:

Firstly, all of San Hiva's current residents were survivors, and that meant they were always wary of strangers.

Secondly, only a small fraction of them actually lived within the town itself. Most had settled down a little east of it; specifically in the area that had belonged to San Hiva's mining company before the Collapse.

Out there lay a long, hangar-like building with walls of corrugated iron plates that had previously housed miners. For the same reason, it had plenty of beds and a large generator that—not surprisingly—ran on coal. And since there was only a single dirt road with two or three sharp bends between this and a large crater with massive piles of coal, that generator was nothing short of a miracle, life being as it was now.

Behind the corrugated iron building was a large,

paved parking lot on which a bunch of trailer homes and caravans had been put up—presumably as makeshift housing for miners after they ran out of space in the main building.

It was in one of these trailers that Rose had made the home she was about to share with David. But the move—which should have been the big topic of the day—didn't take up much space in any of their heads when Randall and Tommy parked their vehicles outside the young couple's future residence.

"I'm sorry," Randall said as they got out of the cars, and he caught David's eye. "But I'll probably have to go over there and talk to him right away."

He nodded towards one of the caravans across the parking lot—one that was framed by a fence and had a large sign next to the door displaying the text: *YES, YES, THE WORLD HAS ENDED, BUT YOU CAN STILL KNOCK FIRST!*

David followed Randall's gaze and nodded.

"It's okay," he said. "It's more important."

He tried to hide it, and most people probably wouldn't have noticed the hint of disappointment in David's voice. But Randall wasn't most people.

He was, given everything, probably the closest thing David had to a father. And despite the fact that Randall would never admit it—either to himself or to others—David also felt more like a son to him than Billy, sometimes.

"Rose, would you ..." he began, but when he turned toward her, he saw that she was already one step ahead of him. She had grabbed the handles of Billy's wheelchair and was turning it around so she could roll him over to the trailer.

Maybe you should reconsider moving with them over here? Allie suggested in his mind. *When David's gone, she won't come running to play nanny all the time. Then all the help you'll have left is Tommy.*

He pushed the thought away and gave Rose a grateful look instead. She smiled, nodded, and then started pushing the wheelchair. However, she didn't make it far, because at the same time Billy pulled the brakes and locked one of the wheels.

"No, w-with," he growled, pointing over toward Randall. "W-with Dad."

"I'm afraid you can't, honey. I need to talk to Tom about what we found in the valley. You would just get bored. But I'll be back soon, okay?"

Under the visor of the cap, Billy's eyes transformed into two thin lines.

"WITH DAD!" he insisted, and this time the words were pronounced clearly, without the slightest stutter. "WITH NOW!"

Randall—who was equally baffled and embarrassed by the boy's reaction—opened his mouth to tell him there was no need to raise his voice.

But when he looked at Billy and saw him sitting with his arms crossed and his head tilted downwards, so the cap covered his face, he hesitated. Because was the boy actually angry? Or was he just shaken? Scared?

Could that be the explanation? Had Billy in fact picked up and understood far more of what had happened on the way here than he had assumed?

The thought was there, and for a fraction of a second, that explanation felt so right, so *indisputable*, that it shook Randall.

"On second thought, I'll take him, Rose," he said. "You've got plenty on your plate here."

"Are you sure?" Rose asked, and when Randall

nodded, she pulled a napkin out of her pocket and wiped some drool off Billy's chin. Then she drove the wheelchair over to him.

Meanwhile, Randall looked at Tommy.

"Do you want to come?"

The question was purely rhetorical, as Randall knew Tommy wasn't going to come. This had a simple reason: the man Randall was going to speak with was one of the authorities in San Hiva. And Tommy wasn't, neither before nor after the Collapse, prone to playing nice with authorities.

Therefore, it wasn't surprising that he responded with a scornful snorting sound and then turned his back to his brother.

A minute later, Randall parked Billy's wheelchair a few yards from the caravan's door while he himself walked over to follow the sign's instructions.

Two short knocks and the preparation for a third was all he had time for before the door opened and swung so quickly toward him that he only just avoided it.

A second later, its sender showed up ... but he

didn't look very bothered by having nearly broken his guest's nose.

"What do you want?"

Randall stared in shock at the man in the doorway and was momentarily unable to answer.

Thomas Longhorn—better known by his nicknames, *Mayor Tom* or just *the Mayor*—was a small, broad-shouldered man with coarse facial features and a scalp which, apart from a single cluster of cork brown hair, was completely bare. In Randall's eyes, Tom's appearance had always been a bit of a mystery, as he looked both harmless and dangerous at the same time. Like some absurd genetic fusion between comedian Jon Lovitz and action movie hero Jason Statham.

And at this moment, it was the latter look that dominated. He looked like someone ready to kick some ass. And like someone who had been under a lot of pressure.

"Hi Tom," Randall said. "I'm sorry if this is a bad time, but we've made a discovery that we need to discuss with you. Well, probably with everybody in charge, actually."

The Mayor stared at him for a long time while the wrinkles in his forehead worked hard. Then he sniffed and nodded towards his dining table inside the caravan.

"Why don't you start by telling me about it," he growled. "Then we'll see."

This arrogant *I'll assess whether it's important enough to involve the others* attitude poked at something in Randall, and he had to swallow a snide response that landed on his tongue. Over time he had learned to distinguish between which fights were worth having with the dear Mayor and which weren't. This belonged in the latter category. In addition, he also had one more thing on his agenda before he walked in the door.

"Is it okay if I bring him?" he asked, pointing his thumb back toward Billy. "He wanted to come with me, and ... well, the others are unloading the truck."

The Mayor glanced at Billy, then over at David, Tommy, and Rose, who were carrying boxes into the trailer, and then back at Billy.

"It's too wide. Can't fit in the doorway."

It wasn't exactly a rejection, but very close. That wasn't surprising, however, because although he had never admitted it directly, the Mayor wasn't among those who saw it as a miracle that Billy—as the only child—had survived his stay in a hospital. He was—and had always been—wary of the boy. But Randall knew this very well, which is why he had his answer ready.

"I'll lift him out of it and carry him in."

The Mayor gave him a disapproving look, but then shrugged and waved them in.

After carrying Billy in, Randall placed him in an office chair at a small folding desk in the middle section of the caravan. Next, he took a seat opposite the Mayor on the horseshoe-shaped plastic bench belonging to the dining table.

On the wall above the Mayor's head hung a row of cabinets close to the ceiling. One of the sliding doors was slightly open, and in the crevice Randall could see the frame and a bit of the screen of an old Panasonic television.

For a moment, he couldn't take his eyes off it. It seemed to be something foreign. Something that didn't belong in this world at all—and it actually gave him the very special sense of déjà vu you get when you see something and feel like you've dreamed about it.

Had things really changed that much? To the point where an old television was such a peculiarity that it seemed—

"BAM!"

The cabinet's door slid shut with a sharp smack. The Mayor had pushed the plate from the other end, and he now gestured for Randall to stop wasting his time and start talking.

"We saw something on our way over here," Randall said. "Out in the woods east of Gleamsdale. A lot of police officers. Dead."

"So, someone wanted revenge," the Mayor suggested, nodding thoughtfully. "It's foolhardy, but far from the first time. And I guess it's somewhat understandable. Many have seen their loved ones get slaughtered by ..."

"No, you misunderstand me," Randall interrupted, knowing it was rarely a good idea to do. "We're talking about *a lot* of cops. *A lot*."

The Mayor squinted, but he didn't say anything.

"There's something else, too," Randall continued. "They ... um, they seemed to have done it themselves."

"What do you mean?"

"Suicide. Or *mass* suicide, I guess would be the technical term. Half of them had shot themselves, while the rest seemed to have thrown themselves off a ledge."

The Mayor stared at him with big eyes and a half-open mouth that looked as if his jawbone had somehow got stuck. In other circumstances, Randall would have found such an expression comical, but right now there was nothing entertaining about it.

"Why ... would they do that?" the Mayor managed to cough out.

Randall shrugged.

"That's what we're wondering. David suggested they might have reached their expiration date. That their bodies no longer could stand to be ..."

"Remote controlled," the Mayor said bitterly.

It wasn't exactly how Randall would have put it,

but it was close enough to make him nod.

Out of the corner of his eye, he noticed Billy spinning around on the office chair by the desk. His first assumption was that the boy was just playing, but then he discovered that Billy had only turned halfway around, before stopping and proceeding to stare intensely at the door they had entered from.

The second after, three short knocks sounded, and Randall felt an icy cold creeping down his back. It was probably just a coincidence, maybe the boy had seen someone outside the window ... but this wasn't the first time something similar had happened. For Billy had lost a lot during his stay at Newcrest Memorial Hospital, yes. But sometimes Randall also had this creeping inkling that the boy had gotten something else in exchange. Something that rarely surfaced—and always made sure to do it so discreetly that it could be interpreted as a coincidence.

But he did stare at the door just before the first knock came. Just as he asked to be rolled in from the terrace a few days ago, minutes before the weather unexpectedly changed and the rain started to pour.

"Hold your horses, I'm coming!" the Mayor growled. However, he only managed to get halfway up from the chair before the door was opened from the outside.

"Marlon? What's up?"

Marlon—a flimsy, older gentleman with thin, white hair that always made Randall think of the artificial cobwebs you put up around Halloween—stuck his head in and smiled in a strained manner.

"I'm sorry to barge in like this," he said. "But we got a radio call from Redwater. And I'm afraid it can't wait. It's important."

The Mayor exchanged a glance with Randall and then looked over at Marlon again.

"I *seriously* doubt that it's more important than this."

This callous response caused Marlon's eyes to flutter nervously back and forth between them. Then he narrowed them and stepped forward.

"It *is* important," he repeated, with the certain repressed anger that you hear when someone who has always been an underdog finally stands firm on something. "*Very* important."

The Mayor stared at the skinny man in the doorway long enough for Randall to find the situation uncomfortable, but when Marlon after some time still hadn't given up, the Mayor simply sighed and waved his hand in a *fine then, have it your way* gesture.

"The call was from the leaders of the Redwater group," Marlon said. "They called because one of their cleanup crews found something this morning."

Randall felt a brief tightening in his stomach—and when he looked over to the other side of the table, he felt pretty confident that the Mayor shared that exact sensation.

"I believe it was out by the dam," Marlon continued. "But I'm not a hundred percent sure about that part."

"Hell, Marlon!" the Mayor exclaimed, throwing his hands out to the sides. "Get to the point! What did they find?"

The outburst got Marlon to curl up and shake like a maligned dog. However, he quickly regained his composure. And when he, as he had been told to, got to the point, it was the other two who felt their hands start to shake.

"It was police officers," he said. "Hundreds of them. Dead."

chapter 7

Like most other groups of survivors, the San Hiva camp had preserved certain elements of democracy from before the fall of civilization and elected some people, including the Mayor, to act as decision-makers on minor things.

If, on the other hand, major concerns arose, carrying consequences for all the inhabitants of the camp, that privilege was immediately waived. In such cases, a town meeting was held so that everyone's opinions could be heard. This was one of the few advantages of the new world. Democracy could be realized in its pure, ideological form.

No one doubted that the discovery of the dead officers called for such a meeting. There was also no need to make an official call for a meeting, as word of the two finds spread like wildfire, and less than two hours after Randall's visit to the Mayor, the entire population of San Hiva had gathered in the square in front of the large, hangar-like building.

There they stood now, faintly buzzing, exchanging theories and anxious glances as the Mayor climbed onto the impromptu speaker's podium; a wooden table with fixed benches on each side.

Randall had also been offered a spot up there, as he was the one who brought the news, but he had turned it down. He preferred to stay with Billy down in the crowd, and besides, he had never really liked being the center of attention. In the past, he usually had to be dragged to the events his publishers planned in connection with his book releases. Back then, few things could put his stomach in knots like the prospect of a book signing.

Stressing over writing your own name. With pay. Christ, you were one privileged son of a bitch.

"Can you all hear me?" the Mayor asked from the bench podium. "Let me know if you can't."

Some in the crowd answered the question with words, but the majority just nodded.

"Oh, that's fucking grand. How are they supposed to let him know if they can't hear him?"

The nasal voice delivering this rather mediocre attempt at a joke belonged to Jack Brackett. He was one of the members of Tommy's cleanup crew, and he was also—Randall had sensed after only knowing him for a short period of time—a bit of an asshole. The kind of person who got a kick from getting on other people's nerves.

For some reason, people like that always felt drawn to Tommy. He attracted them like flypaper, and then, when he started hanging out with them, their idiocy began to rub off on him too.

And the cleanup crew had not just one, but several of the same type, so when they hung out and played poker after dragging corpses and digging graves all day long, it was like submerging Tommy in a bathtub filled with bad influence in liquid form. Almost literally, as there usually was a good stack of empty bottles on the table when such an evening was over. And even though Randall wasn't the gambling type, he'd be willing to bet some money that Jack probably had a little alcohol coursing through his veins right now. At least that's what it sounded like.

"You've probably heard the rumors already," the Mayor continued. "But just to make it clear, I can tell you that two mass graves have been discovered."

While the news was probably not actual *news* to anyone, a unanimous sigh of surprise—and resentment—spread through the crowd.

"The dead, apart from a few people, are almost exclusively police officers. And it needs to be thoroughly investigated, of course, but ... so far it seems they have done it themselves. That it was mass suicide."

"Why would they do that?" asked a man in the front row. "Why would they throw away their highest card like that?"

Randall exchanged a glance with Tommy, who had asked a similar question out in the valley.

"That's a fair question, Carl," said the Mayor, nodding to the man. "The honest answer is that we don't know. We have two guesses. One is that their batteries have simply run out and that their last act was to get rid of themselves."

He took a short break, probably expecting that someone would ask for a clarification of that explanation.

But—and this was in some way a very scary thing for Randall to realize—no one appeared to be in doubt about what the Mayor meant. Despite it being a taboo subject, there apparently was a fairly similar perception of what had been wrong with the officers. That something had *controlled* them.

"Our second guess is that they have been discarded because ..."

The Mayor hesitated, a little *too* long, and this could be sensed so clearly in the crowd that it almost felt as if their fear and worry had taken on a physical shape. That it had become something you could reach your hand out and touch.

"Just say it!" sounded Jack's nasal—and drunken—voice. "They sacked the cops because they couldn't finish the job and exterminate us completely. So now they're probably gonna send something even worse."

Shut up before you start a panic, Randall thought,

but even though part of him wanted to go over and scream just that into Jack's face, he didn't. He knew it would only be met with some stupid hillbilly insult. Besides, he didn't want to get into a fight when he had Billy sitting in the wheelchair right in front of him. So, instead he looked over at his older brother, who was standing next to Jack, and asked him wordlessly to get his loud-mouthed buddy under control.

Tommy poked Jack with his elbow to catch his attention—and when he had it, he slowly shook his head.

For a moment Jack stared at him with both his shoulders pulled back and a challenging smile on his lips. Then he grabbed the bottom edge of his shirt and pulled it out, as if with its printed picture—a big yellow smiley—he wanted to tell Tommy to relax. That it was just a joke.

But at least he did shut up.

"Panic and unfounded theories are the last things we need right now," said the Mayor, letting a serious glance slide over the crowd from his place on the wooden bench. "But yes, obviously, we have to consider the possibility that there may be ... something else on the way."

"Dear God," Randall heard a woman's voice whispering somewhere behind him—and somewhere farther ahead in the crowd the answer came: "A waste of time, lady. He ain't answering the phone anymore. He's up there playing golf or something."

"But either way, it's important that we prepare ourselves in the best possible way," the Mayor continued. "And that brings me to the next item. We need some volunteers to go to the riverbed where they were found. A scavenging team, if you will. It's not a fun task, I know, but we can't ignore the fact that there's a large arsenal of firearms and ammunition out there, just lying around. And one thing's for sure: if we don't take those weapons, somebody else will."

He paused rhetorically, giving the crowd time to let that scenario—and its possible consequences for the San Hiva camp—sink in. Then he spoke again, even louder and with a more authoritarian tone.

"Are there any volunteers?"

"Sign me up!" sounded somewhere a little farther to the right of where Tommy and Jack stood. "I've already been out there once."

It was Rose. She stood with her hand in the air and a steely look in her eyes. David was by her side, watching her with a perplexed expression on his face. But he neither contradicted her nor protested. Instead, he started raising his arm as well.

He did, however, only manage to get it halfway up before Jack Brackett's voice burst through.

"Fuck it, if I can team up with little Rose, I'm in too!" he shouted, waving one arm over his head as he ran over and squeezed in next to Rose. He then leaned—way too close—in towards her and whispered something in her ear.

Randall was too far away to hear the words, but the look on Rose's face, as well as the swear word her lips shaped, told him more than enough.

Yes, Jack Brackett certainly did get a kick out of being an asshole, especially towards women—and now he topped it off by pinching Rose's buttocks with his fingers.

Christ, if David saw that ...

No further did Randall get with his stream of thought, because yes, David had seen it. And within a fraction of a second, he had grabbed the collar on Jack's shirt and was dragging him away.

"Oh, for God's sake," Randall muttered, after which his gaze fell down onto the wheelchair, the handle of which his hands rested on. He didn't want to let it go, but he couldn't spot anyone who ...

Oh, fuck it. He let go of the handles, turned around, and began to move in a zig-zag pattern through the crowd.

"David! David, let him go!"

David didn't hear him. Or *chose* not to hear him. In any case, his attention was focused on Jack, whom he still half-pushed, half-pulled with him.

And, of course, Jack's reaction to the situation—which people like him often resort to for inexplicable reasons—was to put on a stupid grin.

"Tommy, help me here, will you?" Randall said as he passed his brother.

It took a moment for Tommy to grasp what was going on—and another one before he actually reacted and came along.

By the time they caught up with David, he had already dragged Jack all the way out of the crowd and thrown him on the ground. There he lay now, cursing—and, absurd as it was, still sporting that idiotic smile on his lips—while David pulled his arm backward and clenched his fist.

Had Randall and Tommy been just a second slower, that fist would probably have landed right in the middle of Jack's face, perhaps even resulting in a broken nose. But at the last second, the two brothers managed to grab David from opposite sides and hold him back.

"Let me go!" David sneered, trying to pull free. In fact, he did manage to get Tommy to lose his balance and stumble. Randall, on the other hand, was successful in both maintaining and tightening his grip. And while doing so, he pulled David closer so he could speak to him without the growing audience behind them being able to listen in.

"David, you need to calm down," he whispered.

"But he always does shit like that. Not only to Rose, but to every—"

"I know," Randall said. "And I'm not saying he doesn't deserve it. But take a look around and think about it. These are your future neighbors. Whatever you choose to do now *will* have consequences, for you and for Rose. And that little prick isn't worth it, is he?"

"The fucking psychopath just jumped me," Jack complained on the ground behind them. "I didn't *do* nothing, man!"

Randall ignored him—and to his relief he saw David do the same.

"Tommy?" Randall said, reaching his hand out to his older brother, who was still lying where David had knocked him down. "Would you get your buddy out of here, please?"

Tommy took his hand and let himself be pulled up ... but hardly had he gotten on his feet before he stumbled and almost fell down again.

For a split second, Randall thought Tommy might have been hit by David's elbow or had hurt his head when he fell. Then he got a glimpse of his eyes, red and slightly foggy, and suddenly it became clear to him that the explanation was quite different.

"What the hell, Tommy. Have you been drinking?"

Tommy uttered one of his *what are you raving about*? snorts and stared at him with an outrage so phony that it was on the verge of being downright pathetic. And then—instead of answering the question—he bent down and helped Jack up.

Randall looked inquiringly over at Rose, who had just now caught up with them and stood with her boyfriend's hands in hers.

She shrugged.

"The two of them went over to Jack's trailer when we finished unloading the boxes. That's all I know."

Randall nodded and then made eye contact with his older brother again.

"Just get that jerk out of here. We'll talk about this later."

"Hey, who are you calling a jerk?" Jack sneered, but his protests died out as soon as Tommy started dragging him away.

And when Jack's nasal voice could no longer be

heard, Randall realized that no other sounds could either.

More than sixty people were standing behind his back—and all of them were silent as the grave.

He took a deep breath and turned around. Sure enough, sixty sets of curious eyes, all aimed at him and David.

"It was just a heated disagreement," he said, holding his hands up apologetically. "A misunderstanding, really. It's over now."

At the edge of the crowd stood a large, gritty man with tousled hair and a full beard. His arms were crossed, and the eyes in his weather-beaten face were directed at David, whom he now slowly began to walk towards.

David was clearly uncomfortable with the situation, but he met the man's gaze and didn't let his eyes shy away. And when Randall instinctively took a step forward to place himself between the two, David discreetly raised his hand and stopped him.

It probably wouldn't have made much of a difference anyway. That big loaf of meat would probably have waded right through him without blinking.

Now the man stopped, less than a yard from David. There he stood, completely still, for a moment. Then he put his hand out.

David stared at it with the distrust that you'd expect to find in a man who is offered a bottle with a picture of a black skull on the label. But he ended up taking and shaking it.

"Don't worry about it," the big man said, exposing a yellowish-brown set of teeth. "You're not the first to grab Jack by the collar ... and you sure as hell aren't going to be the last."

David nodded, then let go of the big man's hand and cast a relieved glance at Randall. One that said: *Holy crap, I thought he was going to rip off my arms or something.*

Randall, equally relieved, wiped his forehead and nodded at him.

"Are we ready to move on with the meeting?" the Mayor asked from the podium.

"Yep, you just go ahead, Tom," said the big man, pointing his thumb towards the corner of the trailer where Tommy and Jack had disappeared a moment ago. "The sideshow freak is gone."

"All right, then. Where did we get to? Oh yes, volunteers. Does anyone else wish to sign up?"

Randall and David exchanged a glance and then both raised a hand.

"David and I would like to join the party. We also helped find it, so we know what we're getting into."

He hesitated, casting a glance back over his shoulder. Then he added:

"And put my brother in our group too."

"It's Tommy, isn't it?"

"Yeah. Tommy Morgan."

The Mayor looked down at a woman who was standing next to the podium bench, writing the volunteers' names on a pad. She did it very slowly and with a neatness that would have driven most people mad. The Mayor, however, waited patiently for her to finish.

When the woman finally nodded, he turned his attention back to the crowd and continued his search for volunteers, but at that point Randall was no longer listening. His focus was solely on the crowd, which he was staring into with a growing unease in his stomach.

They weren't as closely packed as before, so he could easily see in between the clusters. The only problem was that the one person he was looking for wasn't anywhere to be seen.

"Hey, Randall, what happened before with Jack, it ... um, I'm sorry. I overreacted, and you saved me from a real crappy situation. So ... yeah, *thanks* is what I'm trying to say, I guess."

"Sure, David," Randall replied, without empathy and without moving his gaze from the crowd. "You're one of the Morgans now. I told you. But listen, have you seen Billy? I can't find him."

David narrowed his eyes. Next to him, Rose did the same. Then they both shrugged their shoulders.

"Could he have rolled back to my ... to our place?" Rose asked.

After the last three words in which she corrected herself, David sent Rose a devoted glance and gave her hand a squeeze. A loving gesture that would normally have warmed Randall's heart, but which he right now found both annoying and inappropriate.

"You'll double-check here," he ordered, pointing towards the crowd. "Then I'll run back to Rose's trailer and see if he's there."

The two young people nodded obediently, then let go of each other's hands and jogged in the direction of the crowd. His commanding tone—and the growing panic in his voice, which no longer let itself be concealed—had clearly frightened them.

But there was no time to worry about small things like that.

Not now, when it felt like his worst nightmare was coming true.

chapter 8

When he closed the trailer door behind him after finding that Billy wasn't in there, Randall's worry turned to fear. And when he returned to Rose and David, both of whom answered the question in his eyes with a resigned shake of their heads, the fear turned into outright horror.

For if you peeled off all layers, leaving only the truth and Randall's exposed soul, there was nothing else left.

Nothing but Billy.

It was the desire to see his son—the desire to save him, to be a *father* to him—that had held him together when the world crumbled around him. It was Billy who had kept him alive back then, and it was, although he wasn't proud of it, probably also Billy who had kept him alive until now.

And now, Billy was gone.

"Where's Tommy?" Rose asked. "Could Billy have gone with him?"

Randall heard her ask the question, but his brain felt like it had suffered a temporary meltdown and he found himself unable to do anything other than stare blankly at her.

"Tommy went with Jack," David replied, pointing in the direction they had gone. "We would have seen it if Billy went with them."

"He knows better," Randall heard himself say in a voice he could barely recognize as his own. "He knows better than to leave without telling me first. So, where the hell *is* he?"

He was aware of how accusatory he sounded and how unfair it was, but he could no more control it than he could make the gray clouds in the sky go away with the mere power of thought.

David and Rose stared at him; both silent, and both with the same compassionate look in their eyes.

Something touched his shoulder, making him jolt. He turned around.

The person who had poked his shoulder and now pulled her hand away was Martha Hymnwell. She was one of the San Hiva camp's oldest members—and a lady he had always had a good feeling about though he didn't know her that well.

"Oh my, I'm very sorry," she said. "I didn't mean to scare you, but I couldn't help but overhear your conversation. Is it your boy you're looking for? The one in the wheelchair?"

"Have you seen him?"

Martha shrugged and smiled.

"Well, yes and no," she said. "I didn't see *him*, per se. But I saw his chair."

"His chair? The wheelchair?"

"Yes, exactly. Most of these meetings go right over the head of an old crow like me anyway, so I went over to check on the chickens. From there you can see all the way to the Radio House and I'm pretty sure I saw his wheelchair parked by the fence over there."

"Thank you, Martha," Randall said, giving the old woman's hand a quick squeeze before turning his back to her and running toward the southwestern part of the camp where the Radio House was located.

The Radio House was, as the first part of its name suggested, San Hiva's communication center, from which they could get in contact with the other camps via an old shortwave radio. Where the name misled a bit, however, was the term *house*. Because the Radio House, like most buildings here, had more in common with a shipping container than a traditional house.

Without a doubt, it was also San Hiva's most isolated building, as it stood alone some distance along the dirt road leading up to the mine and the coal crater. There it had been built on top of a hill, undoubtedly to ensure the best possible signal for the radio antenna, which was its only company.

Both the Radio House and the antenna were enclosed behind a metal fence of the type that typically surrounds military bases, and in the middle of that fence hung a large yellow warning sign.

NO TRESPASSING!

It was in front of this sign Randall saw him. Little fair-haired Billy with the red cap and the striped shirt. His little bumblebee, who—instead of the symbolic wings that life should have given him—had gotten a chair with wheels.

A chair that he, contrary to what Martha had said, was sitting in right now. Her old eyes must have played tricks on her.

"What on Earth are you doing, hon?" Randall said as he slid to his knees and put his arms around his child. "Why are you out here all alone? Are you okay? You can't just run off like that, you hear? We couldn't find you anywhere. I need you to tell me when you leave. Always. I was worried sick."

He heard himself, heard the words—a mash of questions and rebukes—gushing out, and he was aware that he didn't give the boy a chance to answer any of it.

But it was okay. Because like all other worried parents who had reacted in the same way, it wasn't really words he let out right now. It was the accumulated emotions. The fear.

"A-away," the boy muttered into his father's shoulder, and Randall held him even tighter.

"Yeah, hon. You were gone. We couldn't see you

anywhere."

Billy shook his head and pulled back a bit. Then he directed his blue eyes—serious and sad—at his father.

"No, not m-me. You. You g-gone."

The place in Randall's heart that had been occupied with worry and fear a moment ago was now filled by another feeling: shame.

Shame for having let go of the wheelchair's handle and leaving his son alone in the middle of a crowd of strange faces. Shame for abandoning Billy to aid David who was not, after all, his own flesh and blood.

"I'm sorry, Billy. I really didn't mean to abandon you like that."

For a while, Billy didn't say anything. He just sat, staring absently towards the ground. Only when the wind made the half-open door to the Radio House clatter did he briefly look up.

But then he suddenly straightened his back and leaned sideways in the wheelchair seat while smiling at his father.

"S-scared?"

Randall had to swallow a lump in his throat before he was able to return the smile.

"Yes, Billy. I was very scared."

chapter 9

The volunteers' trip out to the valley and riverbed was postponed twice—and in both cases the reason was the same.

The first signs of the storm's arrival came on the very first night after the meeting in San Hiva, and when Randall looked out the window of Billy's room that night—after once again being woken up by the high-pitched tones of the panic bell—he knew it right away: this was going to be one of the bad ones.

He was right. The storm tore several roof tiles loose on Tommy's farm, and it filled the backyard as well as the driveway with broken branches and leaves. In fact, one of the largest branches would probably have gone straight through the wind-shield of Tommy's truck if it had landed just half a yard further to the left.

Since the storm hadn't calmed down the next morning, it wasn't really a surprise when the radio call from San Hiva came in. Understandably, none of the volunteers felt like trotting around in a steep wooded area while the worst storm of the year shook and pulled the trees around them.

The second cancellation started as a delay, but developed into a call-off, and again it was the stormy weather that was to blame. At least indirectly, as it turned out that the storm had uprooted a large pine tree and tipped it over, so it blocked the entrance to the Denswool tunnel. And of course, the volunteers from San Hiva had no real alternative. They needed to use that tunnel to get out to the area east of Gleamsdale, where the valley and the riverbed were located.

According to David and Rose, twelve volunteers had been out there, and a good handful of them were fresh young men of David's age. Yet it only took the first failed attempt to realize that getting the huge tree trunk off the road would take them all day. This left them with the choice between postponing the weapon-scavenging to another day ... or risk having to wander around in a mass grave while darkness fell.

Of course, since that wasn't exactly a difficult decision, Randall received another radio call—which fortunately came in *before* they left the farm.

Now, early morning on the third day after the meeting, as Randall parked his car—the first in a caravan of four—on the side of the road up on the ridge, it looked like the project would finally succeed. Nothing had blocked the road out there, and apart from a little frost, the weather didn't cause them any problems.

"Wasn't it around here?" Randall asked, catching Rose's eyes in the rearview mirror.

"I think so, but ... yep, it's here. I recognize that dead tree over there."

She pointed to an old, dried-out tree so rotten it was the color of ashes, and Randall noticed the hint of a smile in the corners of her mouth.

"Yep, that's the one," she said. "I gave it a hug last time because I was slipping."

"It's incredible that it's still standing."

"Hey, are you calling me fat?" Rose replied promptly, and now the smile spread to the rest of her mouth. It also rubbed off on David in the backseat next to her.

For Tommy, who was sitting in the passenger seat, Rose's remark on the other hand sparked no reaction at all. His face was completely expressionless. That was nothing new, though. It had been like that more or less all the time since the day when David jumped Jack—and when Randall caught Tommy in getting drunk in the middle of the day, knowing he had an important meeting to go to.

Whether it was anger or a guilty conscience that caused the expressionless face, Randall wasn't sure. Knowing Tommy, it could be both. What he did know, however, was that it wasn't worth starting a conversation about the episode until his older brother's stone face had loosened up a bit.

And so, Randall just ignored it for now and smiled at Rose while loosening his seat belt.

"Oh, come on, Rose. You know what I mean. You're not fat ... you're just big-boned."

Once he had gotten out of his own car, he walked over to the next in line and signaled the driver to roll down the window.

The man behind the wheel—who incidentally was the same big man who had given them a good scare a few days ago and shaken David's hand afterward—stuck out his head.

"Is this the place?"

"We're pretty sure," Randall replied, pointing down towards the slope. "At the bottom of the hill."

Brent, as the big man was called, turned his head and looked in the direction Randall pointed.

"It looks steep."

Randall smiled. It was exactly what Rose had said. And he decided to give Brent the same understated answer she had gotten.

"It looks worse than it is."

Brent cast another glance at it and then frowned.

"Your youngest isn't coming, I suppose."

"My youngest?"

"Yeah, the one in the wheelchair. I don't reckon he'll be able to ... you know, with the hills and all."

"Oh, now I get it," Randall said, smiling. "Billy's not my youngest, he's my *only*. And no, he's not coming today. He's with Rose's neighbor. When she heard that we planned to go to San Hiva this morning so we could all drive together, she offered to look after him today."

Above his tangled beard, Brent's eyes looked completely baffled for a moment. Then the connection began to dawn in them, and he raised his index finger.

"So that one isn't your son?"

"Who? David? No, he's not. Before the Collapse, we didn't even know each other. We met when it all went to hell ... and yeah, I suppose you might say we took him in."

"That's awfully kind," Brent said, nodding thoughtfully. "But I reckon that's how we survive, isn't it? By taking care of each other and sticking together."

His voice had an unreserved awe that made Randall feel a little embarrassed.

"Yes ... yes, I guess it is," he said, clapping his hand awkwardly on the roof of the big man's car.

"But I think we'd better get the rest of the herd together now."

The rest of the herd were the last two groups that had now arrived and parked their vehicles behind Brent's car. Several of them had already stepped out and were walking toward Randall. Two of them—a young guy in his twenties with short-cut hair and a woman old enough to be his mother—were carrying a folded, dark blue plastic tarp.

Bringing that was Randall's suggestion. The idea was that they could fold it out on the ground and gather all the dead officers' service weapons in a pile on top of it. Then all they needed to do was to close it up like a sack in order to carry all the weapons up in one single run.

The idea had been met with praise, and Randall suspected it was at that point he inadvertently ended up wearing the leader's jersey.

In any case, he had somehow gotten the role of the unofficial expedition leader. Should he doubt that, a single look at the other volunteers, who were now huddled together in a semicircle around him, awaiting his commands, would settle the matter.

"It's just down this slope," he said, pointing. "I suggest that a few of us stay up here to keep an eye on the cars."

"Fran and I can do that," replied a woman from the group driving the last car of the caravan. "Then we'll let all the strong young legs trudge down the hill."

"Sounds fair to me," Randall said, looking around at the rest. "Does everyone agree?"

No one protested.

"All right, Fran and ...?"

"Rita," said the woman, giving him a smile.

Randall returned it and winked at her.

"Exactly. Fran and Rita will keep watch up here. David, do we have a gun they can borrow?"

"No need," Rita said, pulling up her woolen sweater so the Browning sitting tucked into her trousers came into view.

Randall raised his hand defensively as if to say: *Fair enough, I'll keep quiet, you're on top of this*. Then he turned to face the rest of the group.

"I won't say this is going to be the worst thing you've ever seen. We all know that would probably be a lie ... unfortunately. But I would still recommend that you take a moment to prepare yourselves mentally. Because we're talking about a mass grave, and while most of us probably won't exactly mourn the cops down there, it isn't for the faint of heart."

This warning was the only words he had prepared—and he expected someone to find them a little overdramatic. That some smart-ass would brag about this being nothing compared to what they'd seen at the beginning when all hell broke loose.

But there was no smart-ass. Everyone was silent. Even Jack Brackett, who stood by the side of the road, smoking a cigarette with Tommy some distance from the others, had nothing to offer.

As the silence reached its natural end, Randall looked over to Rose and David, both of whom nodded. Then he took a step forward and said:

"All right, let's get this over with. You know what you're looking for. Weapons, ammunition, and whatever else that might be of interest goes on the tarp. Rose and David here are in charge from now on, and they'll show us the way."

With those words, he handed over the invisible leader's jersey to the two young people, who, without saying anything, waved the groups with them and began the descent down the slope.

Randall found a spot in the rearguard, where he accompanied Brent and a woman whose face he recognized but whose name he couldn't remember.

Brent, however, he had no trouble remembering, as he had made quite an impact on him. Not just because of the thing with David and the handshake, but also because there was something about the big man that reminded him of one of his old friends. In truth, he wasn't quite sure why that was, as Brent didn't look like Joel at all. Not regarding his physical appearance, anyway. Joel wasn't even close to being such a big loaf of meat as ...

Suddenly he knew what it was. It was the *calm*. Brent had the same relaxed demeanor as Joel had. The natural ease and calm which Randall had benefited greatly from when he and Allie broke up, and he was on the ropes. Back then, Joel was an invaluable support.

Oh, God, that was a long time ago. Heck, Joel wasn't even Joel anymore. The last time Randall saw his old buddy was the day he returned from the cabin in Maiden Lake—to a world that had lost its mind. That day, he came across Joel and Kirsten outside Carol's Diner.

Both were blank.

"What the hell were you up to that day?"

For a moment, Brent's question caused Randall to stiffen and stare dumbfoundedly at him, thinking he might have somehow read his mind and that it was Joel and Kirsten he asked about.

"What ... what do you mean?"

"The day you found the dead cops," Brent elaborated. "What the hell were you doing down here?"

Randall shook his head and had to suppress a smile.

"It was my son," he said. "He lost his baseball cap. The rear window of the car was open, and the wind grabbed it. So, we pulled over to find it."

Brent looked back over his shoulder and afterward down the slope. Then he let out a whistling sound between his lips.

"That far? Really?"

"Yeah, it was pretty bad luck, I guess."

"You can say that again. I mean ... hey, what's going on down there? They're whipping around like a bunch of wild geese."

Randall followed Brent's gaze and immediately understood what he meant.

The front group, now having reached the bottom, were waving their arms feverishly up and down. Clearly, they were upset by something.

"What's happening?" he shouted down to the nearest group.

"No idea."

"I'm going take a look, okay?" Randall said, and without waiting for a response from Brent, he started jogging down the slope.

He didn't like this. Especially not now, when he spotted Rose and David. They looked just as strung up as the others.

"What's going on?" he asked again as he caught up with the next of the scattered clusters. "What did they find?"

This time he got an answer—but it wasn't a

reassuring one.

"They're saying that someone beat us to it. That all the weapons are gone."

chapter 10

"I knew we couldn't trust those fucking assholes in Redwater. I just *knew* it!"

In all probability, he wasn't aware of it himself, but this frustrated outburst from Jack caused a fear that had been lying dormant in Randall's consciousness to break through the surface and stick out its ugly head.

And he wasn't alone in feeling it. He could read this very clearly in the faces of many of the others.

The fear was simple and concrete, and it undoubtedly was a result of the myriad of post-apocalyptic films and series that were trending right before the world actually *did* come to an end.

In those, the pattern was always the same: the world ended, only a few survived—and before long, the lack of resources had these survivors going at each other's throats.

Give or take a few minor details, this was also the image in the minds of most survivors when the police force's first massacre was over and they had a moment to catch their breath. Therefore, it was a relief for many to discover that reality was actually different. That the common tragedy and having a common—albeit invisible—enemy made the survivors stand together, rather than fight each other.

They were divided into camps, yes, but they talked, they shared what there was to share, and they helped each other when needed.

That sense of unity—and the trust it required—had at this moment been seriously tested, which Jack almost perfectly summed up when he shouted that they should never have trusted the fucking assholes in Redwater.

In those words, he briefly and accurately gave the enemy something it hadn't had before:

A face. *The assholes in Redwater*. The only ones, besides the San Hiva camp, who knew about the dead policemen in the riverbed.

But was that proof enough? Randall wasn't sure.

After all, the storm was still a factor, and he simply couldn't imagine the people of Redwater being so desperate to steal the weapons that they would risk their lives by braving the storm.

"Just wait and see. Before long, they'll be showing up in San Hiva, armed to the teeth, demanding our cattle!"

Randall looked over at Jack and then at Tommy.

"Can you make him shut up?"

For a moment Tommy seemed ambivalent, which Randall suspected was because on the one hand he wanted to help and on the other wanted to keep up his stone face for a while longer. He ended up biting his lip and sighing.

"I'll talk to him."

"Thank you."

"Mm, whatever."

With those words, Tommy went over to Jack, grabbed his arm, and pulled him aside. Meanwhile, Randall moved—carefully, so as not to step on any of the bodies—toward the center of the valley, where David sat on his knees, staring down at one of the dead officers.

"Do you think he's right?" he asked when he looked up and spotted Randall. "Do you think Redwater would screw us over like that?"

"Jack is an idiot," Randall replied.

"You're not wrong on that ... but do you think he could be right on this?"

Randall thought for a moment, then shook his head.

"No. It doesn't add up. First off, it would be just as difficult for them to get out here with the storm, and second, they have their own mass grave. We have to assume that it was also full of guns."

David picked something up from the ground to the left of the dead officer's violet face, studied it for a moment, and then threw it away again.

"Who, then?"

Randall had no answer and had to shrug his shoulders.

"But we'll have to figure it out in a hurry, right?" David continued. "Otherwise, we've got another problem on our hands. A *big* one."

Randall let his eyes wander across the faces of the volunteers. As they stood there, scattered clusters of living people in a sea of dead, each and every one of them looked anxious and exhausted.

And in almost all of their eyes, he saw the same poisonous question David had asked him a moment ago.

Could Jack be right? Could the Redwater group be responsible for this?

part 3

ASSHOLES & GRAVEROBBERS

"Oh yes, the face of fear is far uglier

than that of the Grim Reaper.

For it has what his has not.

Two eyes and a tongue."

— O. E. *Geralt,* Listen Carelessly.

chapter 11

By the time the caravan with the volunteers returned to the camp in San Hiva a little later in the day, Tommy's noisy poker-buddy had calmed down a bit.

But despite this small miracle—that Jack Brackett had shut up for once in his life—the damage had been done. His unproven postulate had taken root, and Randall could almost see how the rumor spread like cancer cells throughout the camp.

Part of him wanted to run away from it. To pick up Billy, drive home to the farm, and never again look back over his shoulder in this direction. To focus solely on his own family, as he had done so far, and let the headaches of San Hiva be the headaches of San Hiva.

The only problem was that there were two

people here he considered part of his family, and he knew that Rose wasn't going to turn her back on this place. Which meant David couldn't be persuaded to do so either.

Hell, Randall wasn't even convinced that Tommy would accept it without protest. After all, he too had made bonds with people in this camp. Not necessarily bonds that were healthy for him, but definitely bonds he wouldn't be eager to cut.

Bottom line? The camp's problem was also Randall's problem, so he decided he'd better talk to the Mayor. But first, there was something else he had to do. Something he had decided just over a year ago should always be his first priority.

With that thought in his mind, he headed over to Rose's neighbor where Billy sat in his wheelchair in the front yard, playing with an old Rubik's cube.

Well, *front yard* was perhaps a rather free definition, since Mary, as the neighbor was called, lived in a trailer home like Rose, and the fenced-in area in front of it was, like the rest of the parking lot, coated in asphalt. However, there was a little plant life. It came in the form of a few large clay pots with flowers.

Mary was, as you would expect when you saw the pots and the well-kept flowers, a woman well up in years. Just how old she was, Randall didn't know. But she was definitely well past the point where it was okay to ask.

But if there was one thing he had learned from the apocalypse, it was that old age didn't necessarily mean weakness. Many of the elderly, especially the men who had been soldiers in some of the great wars, handled all the macabre events in the beginning far better than the young. As one of them had once told Randall, it took a lot more than a dead man in a lamppost to keep you awake at night once you had seen your soldier buddies getting ripped apart by hand grenades and landmines.

He saw some of the same coolness in the eyes behind Mary's glasses. Even now, as she stood in the doorway to the trailer and watched him with a smile, it was there. Something tough, a survival instinct that hid in the pupils of her otherwise friendly brown eyes.

Truth be told, this was probably the main reason

why she was allowed to look after Billy. Because Randall felt pretty sure that what he saw in those eyes would keep his son safe.

"Hey, BumbleBilly, did you have fun?" he asked, and then, without waiting for an answer, he turned to Mary: "Did he behave?"

Mary tilted her head slightly and looked down at Billy.

"He did. He only ran away once."

"Ran away?"

"Don't worry, it sounds worse than it is. He just took a little ride, probably to get some air. Or a break from all my silly stories."

She exchanged another look with Billy, and both smiled.

"It was just a little trip," Mary repeated. "Couldn't have been more than five minutes. I found him by the medicine depot."

Under normal circumstances, Randall would have had a talk with Billy, explained to him why you couldn't just run away without saying anything.

But right now, he was exhausted and had his

head full of other things, so instead he just walked over to the wheelchair, put his hand on Billy's shoulder, and gave it a squeeze while shaking his head slowly.

"How did it go out there?"

"Not too good, Mary. Someone had already been out there."

"What's that supposed to mean?"

Randall scratched the back of his neck and sighed.

"It was completely raided. A fair guess would be that there were at least fifty handguns out there when we first saw it. Today we went through it meticulously, and we found a total of two pistols and a handful of ammo. One of the guns wasn't even down in the valley. We found it under the seat of one of the patrol cars."

"So that's what all that's about," Mary said, nodding toward the corrugated iron building, where a bunch of the camp's residents stood in scattered groups, talking. "I had a feeling that something was brewing, the way people were buzzing around after you came back."

For a brief moment, the image from before—the cancer cells that spread in the camp—resurfaced before Randall's inner eye, and he nodded.

"Yeah, the popular theory is that the group from Redwater is behind it."

"But you don't agree?"

Randall shrugged.

"I think it's very early—*too* early—to start drawing conclusions."

Mary squinted her eyes and stared at him for a while. Then she nodded over towards the Mayor's caravan at the other side of the parking lot.

"Maybe someone should mention that to him *before* the small groups over there turn into a lynch mob."

Randall nodded.

"Look, Mary, I know it's a lot to ask when you've already had him all day, but—"

"You go ahead. I don't mind, and I don't think Billy does either. Besides, I know Doreen has got an old jigsaw puzzle lying around. Maybe we could borrow that. Doesn't that sound like fun, Billy?"

Billy looked up and smiled, first at her, then at

his father.

"You behave yourself, okay?" Randall said, ruffling the boy's hair. "No running away this time, okay?"

Billy uttered a grunting sound that could just as likely mean *yes* as *no*. Then he reached out his hand.

Randall took it, gave it a squeeze, and then slowly let it go.

"I'll be right over there," he said, looking at Mary. "You just call if you need me."

"We've got it under control. You just go."

Randall took a breath, was on the verge of saying something more, but then decided not to and instead walked straight over toward the Mayor's caravan.

When he got there, he stopped in front of the door and raised his hand to knock, but his knuckles hadn't even touched the door before it was opened from the inside.

"Yeah, I was wondering when you'd show up, Randall. Come in."

Neither the words nor the tone of his voice gave

the impression that the Mayor was the least bit surprised to see him, which confused Randall a little.

"Take a seat," the Mayor said, gesturing toward the same dining table they had sat at last time. "Coffee?"

Randall went—hesitantly and now even more confused—over and sat down on the bench by the table. It wasn't like the Mayor to let him in without a condescending remark or two. And it wasn't like him to offer coffee either. Something was wrong ... and Randall wasn't sure it was just about the missing guns out in the valley.

"Only if you've already got some in the pitcher. No need to brew any for me."

The Mayor nodded, found two cups, and put them on the table. He then picked up a thermos from the desk in the middle of the caravan.

The cup wasn't very clean, and the coffee tasted like rust, but the effect of caffeine was welcome, so Randall didn't complain.

"Someone beat you to it, I heard," the Mayor said.

Randall halfway blew, halfway sighed on his

coffee and nodded.

"Did they put a name on that someone, too?"

The Mayor narrowed his eyes.

"In fact, they did. But I'd like to hear your thoughts."

"Why is it relevant what I think?"

The Mayor thought for a moment and then shrugged.

"You don't live here. You're not in the direct line of fire, so you might be better able to keep your cool."

"Fair enough," Randall said. "Not Redwater. That's what I'm thinking."

"Because?"

"They have no meaningful motive. First of all, you're allies, you trade supplies on a regular basis. Secondly, they found a bunch of dead officers themselves, so we have to assume they aren't short on guns right now. And finally, there's the storm. If we weren't able to get out there before now, it would have been completely impossible for them."

Over the edge of his coffee cup, the Mayor nodded emphatically, as if he could easily follow Randall's thinking.

No, it was more than that. He almost nodded *impatiently*. The way people do when they know in advance what the other one is about to say and just want to move on to the next item on the agenda.

"There's something you're not telling me," Randall said, partly inquiring, partly stating.

The Mayor nodded again and suddenly looked very serious.

"We are not the only ones who were late to the show. We got a radio call while you were gone ... well, actually we got more than one. But one of them was from Redwater. It turns out they also showed up to a mass grave that had been looted. And they ... yeah, I think you can guess the rest."

"They're suspecting you?" Randall said, and when it triggered another nod from the Mayor, he uttered a deep sigh. "And the others?"

The Mayor blinked.

"The others?"

"You said you got more than one radio call," Randall elaborated. "Where were the other calls from?"

"Hollowfolk and Crestmont. In both cases, the

message was the same. They also found mass graves."

"Fuck."

"Yep. That about sums it up. We're talking about four camps so far."

"So... what? Do we dare to think that it's the same everywhere? That all the cops are gone?"

"It looks that way."

Randall took a sip of his coffee and leaned back in the seat. Under him, the seat cushion sighed.

"The question is whether this is good news," the Mayor continued. "Or if this might be when all the survivors start looting and shooting each other, like we all thought they would in the beginning."

"I'd probably wait a bit before rushing out to cheer in the streets," Randall said. "Especially when we don't know what happened with those guns."

Before the Mayor answered, he let his eyes slide toward the window. Behind its glass you could see a piece of the parking lot. On it, two of the smaller groups from earlier had turned into one larger—and seemingly more agitated—group. Just as Rose's neighbor had predicted.

"Street parades are just about the last thing in the world I'm worried about," the Mayor said as he turned his attention back to Randall. "First we have to get past Thursday. Right now, that's my biggest concern."

"Past Thursday?"

The Mayor nodded.

"Just like you said, Redwater is one of the groups we have allied ourselves with and we do exchange resources with them on a regular basis. Medicine and first aid kits from their hospital in exchange for coal from the mine and sometimes maybe a hen or two. That kind of thing. And we've got a shipment coming in from them this Thursday."

"Okay, I see ... but I'm still not sure what it is you want from me?"

The Mayor shrugged and gave him a wry smile, as if to say, *Okay, you got me*.

"It's about your brother."

"Tommy? What has he done now?"

"Nothing. But I've gathered that Jack Brackett is the front man of the rebellion out there. And I know he and your brother are ... well, let's be honest. Calling them *drinking buddies* wouldn't be unfair, would it?"

Once again, Randall's gaze slipped out the back window to the mob, still expanding, and he caught himself thinking he wouldn't want to be in the Mayor's shoes the next couple of days.

"They play the occasional game of Texas Hold'em," he said, sighing. "And yes, there are usually bottles on the table. The booze is something Tommy has struggled a lot with in the past, and with the way the world is now ... well, that doesn't make it any easier."

"Of course not," the Mayor said. "And part of me understands that, believe me, but... "

He lowered his gaze and let it rest on the coffee cup for a moment. When he lifted it again, his eyes were dark with seriousness.

"Jack Brackett is a dumbass," he said. "But he's a *loud* dumbass. Especially when he's had some beers. And right now, he's got a lot of listeners because they're nervous. So, I'd prefer it if there weren't any ... poker nights for that group over the next few days."

"I'll see if I can keep Tommy at home," Randall replied. "Get him to stay on the farm. And if not, I'll talk to him. Explain the situation to him."

"It would be a big help if he could stay away until things have calmed down. Because if Jack can stir up a panic like that now, I'm afraid to even think about what will happen if he steps out to a crowd after a poker night."

Although Randall wasn't too proud of this conversation because he somewhere beneath the surface felt he was deceiving his brother, that image—a drunken Jack Brackett riling up a crowd of frightened people—was extremely convincing.

"I'll see what I can do."

"That's all I ask," said the Mayor. He was smiling, but when he saw Randall start to get up, the smile disintegrated, and he signaled with his hand for him to wait.

"There's one more thing, Randall. Probably nothing, but ..."

"But what?"

"We had some visitors while you were away. Some military personnel."

"Military personnel? I didn't think there was any military left at all."

"None of us did. But apparently, they have a bunker somewhere in Maryland that survived. Some kind of research facility."

Maybe it was just the way the Mayor wrinkled his nose when he said it, but something about that word—*research facility*—set off an alarm in Randall's head.

And it didn't get any better when the Mayor continued:

"That's where they came from, and they were very interested in getting to talk to you and—"

"And Billy," Randall concluded, after which his gaze instinctively went out the window and onto the trailer that belonged to Rose's neighbor, where his son had spent most of the day.

"Don't worry," the Mayor interjected. "Having been on the run from the police for so long, the sight of uniforms isn't exactly something that makes us spread our arms and welcome people. So, we didn't tell them anything, and we made sure they didn't see Billy. I just wanted to warn you, so you're prepared if they decide to show up again."

"I appreciate that, Tom. Really."

The Mayor nodded and tilted his hand in a *don't mention it* gesture. But his eyes still looked like he had something else on his mind. Maybe something he wasn't sure should be said out loud.

"Was there anything else?" Randall asked.

The Mayor looked down at the table.

"Maybe it wouldn't hurt."

"What?"

"If they took a look at the miracle boy out there ... if that's what they came for."

Randall narrowed his eyes and stared—for *a very* long time—at the man across the table. Then he put his hands on the edge and pushed himself up.

"I'll talk to Tommy."

He stood still for a moment to see if the Mayor would ask him to sit down again. But the Mayor constrained himself to a nod while muttering:

"That sounds good, Randall."

chapter 12

Accommodating the Mayor's desire to keep Tommy away from San Hiva turned out to be a much easier task than Randall had expected.

The first few days after they had come home to the farm, he didn't even have to distract his older brother or make up excuses for why it was probably best to stay at home. Because during those days, practically only two things could motivate Tommy to get his ass off the armchair: an empty log basket and an empty stomach.

Part of the reason was, of course, the usual sloth-like laziness that Tommy had honed throughout his long life as a bachelor and had now mastered at an almost Olympic level.

Another reason—and this one gnawed a bit on Randall's conscience—was probably some kind of sadness. After all, Randall wasn't the only one who considered David a part of the family, and of course it also affected Tommy that he had moved out.

Surprisingly, it didn't seem to have had any impact on Billy whatsoever. In fact, he seemed a bit more lively than usual. Several times Randall had seen him milling around the house in his wheelchair ... almost as if the boy wanted to take advantage of the extra space.

Finding a good excuse to keep Tommy at home on the Thursday when the shipment from Redwater was planned to arrive in San Hiva also didn't require any particularly creative effort from Randall. In fact, the excuse came to him, almost like a ready-to-use solution, during a radio call with David. In it, David told him that everything was going fine in the new home ... except that he was a bit worried about Rose as she had been sick again that morning.

Randall had reassured him that it was probably just the season—and at the same time realized that he had just gotten the perfect excuse served to him on a silver platter.

And yes, when Randall told Tommy that Rose was sick and therefore couldn't look after Billy while Randall went to a meeting with the Mayor in San Hiva, he immediately took the job. He even agreed when Randall said it would probably be easier if they just stayed home on the farm.

So, as it turned out, keeping Tommy at home was almost too easy, as all the stars aligned all by themselves.

Unfortunately, not much indicated that the same could be said of the long-awaited Thursday when the shipment from Redwater was to arrive in San Hiva at noon.

Already two hours earlier, when he parked the car in front of Rose and David's trailer, Randall had felt it. Like a strong tension, almost an electrical charge, it lay in the air, and now—ten minutes before noon—it had only gotten stronger.

Nerves, tension, and uncertainty. An extremely dangerous cocktail. Especially if an explosive catalyst like Jack Brackett was added to the mix.

And Jack was present. Randall had seen him sneaking around among the many small clusters of camp members who had spread across the square in front of the corrugated iron building.

Randall was part of one of those clusters. Its other members were Rose, David, and Brent.

"I don't like this. Several of them have brought guns."

Randall looked at Rose, from whom the remark had come, and expressed his agreement with a nod. He had made the same observation and he didn't like it one bit either.

"It's not so much the guns that bother me," Brent said. "It's that they're trying to hide them."

It took a moment for Randall to realize what the big man meant. But when he squinted his eyes and saw one of the men in a group over on the other side pulling down his jacket to cover the gun in his jeans, the penny dropped.

Brent had a point. With the world being as it was, it was completely acceptable to carry a firearm, and no one would raise an eyebrow at the sight of it. Even more than before, it was considered a fundamental right.

So why would anyone make a conscious effort to

hide it... if it wasn't because you had something else to hide?

Or you could simply be overinterpreting because you're a bit more on edge than usual today.

Maybe. But once the question had appeared in his mind, he couldn't let it go—and looking once more at one of the other groups, he discovered something that really set off an alarm:

The Mayor was over there ... but he didn't look like himself. He looked uneasy, tense.

And behind his back—very, very close—stood another man. Randall couldn't remember his name, but he recognized him, and he knew it was one of Tommy's poker buddies.

A friend of Jack Brackett, in other words.

In a movement he hoped would seem calm and natural, Randall snuck over next to David.

"Maybe you should take Rose back to the trailer."

"What do you mean?"

"It's probably nothing, but I'd feel better if you stayed there until we're sure this goes smoothly and peacefully.'

"Okay."

Randall had expected to be met with protest, so this response from David left him completely baffled.

"Okay," David repeated, now both sounding and looking serious. "We'll go home ... *if* you come with us."

"I can't do that. I have something that I need—"

Randall didn't get any further before he was cut off by three different sounds at almost the same time.

One was the sound of an engine and car tires on gravel.

The second was a short whistle, followed by the sound of firearms being pulled out and loaded.

The third sound was Jack Brackett's nasal voice, in a pitch far above the usual, screaming:

"THE GRAVEROBBERS FROM REDWATER ARE HERE! REMEMBER WHAT WE TALKED ABOUT: IF THEY TRY ANYTHING, YOU POP 'EM FIRST AND ASK QUESTIONS LATER!"

chapter 13

Time is relative. Although most people know this sentence and are aware that it has scientific justification, it often feels like an abstract claim.

But there are moments where any doubts about the truth in these words disappear. Moments when time is no longer measured in seconds and minutes, but in glimpses and eternities.

As the truck from Redwater rolled in and parked in front of the crowd of San Hiva residents, Randall Morgan—and likely the majority of the people standing around him—had such a moment.

He stood there, frozen, confused and caught in a moment that at the same time felt endless and as something which could end in a massive explosion at any time.

As if reality were playing out at half-pace, he saw

armed men tightening the grips on their guns and drops of sweat slowly rolling down their foreheads as the focus of their aim stepped out of the truck.

A total of five men. Five brave—or perhaps just foolhardy—men from Redwater who at this moment had about three times as many firearms pointed straight at them.

However, one of the guns wasn't aimed at the guests from Redwater. Because Randall's suspicion from earlier had been right: Jack's poker buddy on the other side did indeed have a gun pressed against the back of the Mayor. Now it had just moved up to his neck instead, and he no longer made any attempt to hide it.

"HANDS WHERE WE CAN SEE THEM! KEEP YOUR FUCKING HANDS WHERE WE CAN SEE THEM!"

Jack's cry cut through the air so eerily clean that it almost sounded unreal, supernaturally loud. That made some sort of sense, though, as there were no other sounds to interfere. Everything was quiet. Like the town square in an old western, just before the final duel between the hero and the villain. The only question was who played which part here.

"Dylan, Mark," Jack continued, now in a slightly calmer voice, but still eagerly waving his hand. "Search them. Make sure they're not carrying any weapons. And look in the back of the truck, too. Make sure there's no one hiding back there!"

"Maybe you should take a breather there, son," said one of the Redwater people; an elderly gentleman in a dark brown suede jacket who Randall recalled had been the first to get out of the truck. "We don't have so many bullets in stock that we'd start throwing them at you for no reason."

Did he just call Jack Brackett son? Randall thought. *This isn't going to end well.*

But no. Whoever this older gentleman was, he either had to have been blessed with luck out of the ordinary or have an immensely good handle on types like Jack. In any case, right now the good Mr. Brackett seemed more confused than angry with his flickering eyes and his half-open mouth.

And it wasn't just Jack who looked disoriented. Behind him, several of his followers had the exact same expression of complete surprise.

"My name is James Whitmoore," the older gentleman declared, and this time he made a point of speaking to everyone in the crowd rather than just Jack. "I'm one of the people who have been elected, *democratically elected*, to make decisions on behalf of the Redwater camp. For this reason, my face will also be new to many of you, as I wouldn't usually be on a trip like this."

He paused and straightened his suede jacket with the same sedateness one in the old world would have expected from a man straightening his Armani suit.

"I chose to tag along today in the hopes that we could resolve the misunderstanding that—

"*Misunderstanding*?" snarled Jack, who had now recovered from the *son* remark and regained his ability of speech. "What *misunderstanding*? You screwed us over and nabbed those guns. Goddamned graverobbers."

At almost every word, he swung the gun up and down, so its barrel alternately pointed down towards the ground and up towards the older gentleman's chest.

And following the last word, *graverobbers*, that was where it stopped, with its aim pointing straight at the center of the man's chest while Jack looked around the crowd.

"Do you hear that? Do you hear how he's trying to play innocent? They must think we're idiots!"

"Yeah, well, you can't really blame them when they come here and see that someone like Jack has been given the floor," Randall heard David muttering behind him.

Whether this was a thought that had simply slipped out, or an attempt to ease a tense situation with a joke, he couldn't tell. But David didn't sound like he saw anything entertaining in this.

Randall got the same impression, looking around at the faces of the crowd. A few of them still nodded, almost in tandem with the tilting gun, when Jack spoke, but the vast majority didn't. In their faces, it was uncertainty that prevailed.

"We're on the same side," said the elderly gentleman in the suede jacket, who had presented himself as James Whitmoore. Again, he was—at least on the surface—completely unaffected by the fact that he was still standing in Jack's line of fire. He ignored him coolly and spoke only to the crowd. "And we're also in the same boat. I don't know how much you've been told, but we also found a mass grave close to Redwater. And it was cleared of weapons, just like yours was."

"And why should we believe that?" Jack tried, but Whitmoore didn't bite. He continued addressing only the crowd in a calm, subdued tone. One that stood in stark contrast to Jack's increasingly uncontrolled voice.

"And to be honest," he said. "We weren't any better than you guys in the first few days. We were frightened and we were confused ... and our first impulse was the same: that it had to be you who were behind it."

He paused, so the image he painted was allowed to settle. Then the lips under his gray-white mustache pulled up in a smile. Not a condescending or *I know better than you* one. Rather one that expressed relief, perhaps even hope.

"But the more we thought about it, the less sense

it made. Because we're allies. Have been, almost since the beginning. So why would you have done it? And *how* could you have done it? Of course, I am referring to the storm."

Whitmoore had the upper hand. You didn't have to have studied rhetoric at Oxford to be able to deduce that. Still, Randall didn't exactly feel calm, looking at the two men.

Maybe it was because Jack's face hadn't changed at all. There were no frowns indicating that he was at least thinking about what the other man said. No movement in the eyebrows. He looked just as stubborn and snappish as when he raised the gun the first time.

Not snappish, Allie corrected in Randall's mind. *Bloodthirsty. That's what he is. Bloodthirsty.*

"Maybe I should go in there?" he heard Rose's bright, melodic voice whisper.

The response came immediately from her boyfriend:

"You're kidding, right?"

"I'm not," Rose said with a touch of irritation in her voice. "I think it might help if I try talking to

Jack. See if I can calm him down."

David stared at her in shock.

"That's a really bad idea."

"Don't be like that. You know Jack likes me. For once, that might be a good thing."

"Hell, Rose. I said *no*!"

Two, maybe three seconds after uttering the last word, David realized what Randall and Brent already knew: he had just ignited a fire inside of his girlfriend—and he hadn't done it with a match. He had done it with a tankful of accelerant and a flamethrower.

"Okay then, I'm going in there," Rose announced, coldly and indisputably, after which she turned her back on all three of them and began to walk over to Jack.

Under normal circumstances, Randall would probably have found this misstep from a beginner in the art of relationships amusing, but the idea that Rose was going into the metaphorical circus ring between the two men, he didn't like. Especially not as the fluctuations from Jack's gun kept narrowing, meaning it spent more and more time aimed directly at Whitmoore.

When Rose stopped a few yards from Jack and made him turn his head by saying his name, Randall noticed a detail in his eyes that caused the hairs on his neck to rise.

Something else had joined the bloodthirsty expression. Something resembling desperation. Like what you'd see in the eyes of an animal that's been surrounded on the savannah ... and is aware of it.

Randall turned around to tell David that they ought to get Rose out of there ... but David wasn't by his side any longer. He was heading toward his girlfriend, who now took a few steps closer to Jack and put a hand on his shoulder.

What she whispered to him, Randall was too far away to pick up, but he did hear Jack's answer:

"But don't you see it, Rose?" he sobbed. "They're graverobbers! F-fucking *graverobbers*! And they'll try to take e-everything from us!"

"We want no such thing, son," Whitmoore replied, but the only answer he got was a raised *I've got this* hand from Rose.

And maybe she would have, if Jack hadn't

spotted her boyfriend rushing toward them—with his hands clenched and at breakneck speed.

But Jack *did* spot David ... and the sight of him did what nothing else until now had been able to do.

It made him point his gun at somewhere other than James Whitmoore's chest.

chapter 14

The events in the seconds leading up to the deafening bang from the gun went by so fast that Randall's brain could barely perceive what was happening.

It was only when he—with the reverberation of the gunshot still ringing in his ears—saw Rose stagger sideways and then fall down on the ground that all the pieces came together: in an attempt to protect her boyfriend, she had jumped in front of the gun at the moment it was fired.

"No, no, no," Jack and David chanted in chorus, with the same panicked confusion in their voices.

It was horrible to listen to. Like a scratched CD, they were stuck, monotonously repeating this one word over and over again. And they kept it up, humming it like some bizarre mantra—Jack while he was being dragged away by two men, and David while he fell to his knees next to his girlfriend.

Without hesitation—and without caring if he pushed the people around him—Randall made his way through the crowd, which seemed intent on holding him back. They got in his way, blocked him, closed in around him like a straitjacket.

When he finally made it to the inner circle, David was no longer the only one squatting next to Rose. Whitmoore and one of the other men from Redwater had joined him.

Whitmoore sat with a gentle but determined grip on David's arm, holding him back. The other sat with his left hand behind Rose's neck and the right pressed against her hip.

It was red, that hand.

Reluctantly, Randall's gaze moved further up. Up to Rose's freckled, always-smiling face.

It was pale, but ... oh, thank God, her eyes were open. She was conscious.

"JONATHAN!" roared the man with his hand on her stomach. "ARE YOU LISTENING? GET IN THE BACK AND FIND ME SOME BANDAGES, SOME ALCOHOL AND SOME ANTIBIOTICS! NOW!"

Over on the left side of the truck, the young man with the long, blond hair that had to be Jonathan jolted as if he'd just woken up. Then he ran to the back of the truck.

When he returned, he carried a box filled with bandage rolls, bottles, and pills. He put it down next to the man with his hand on Rose's stomach.

The man rummaged through the box with his free hand, pulled up a bottle, unscrewed the lid with his teeth, and used its contents to clean the wound.

Meanwhile, Randall sat down next to David and put his hand on his shoulder. It was quivering.

"I ... am okay, you know," Rose stammered when she spotted Randall. "Tell him, will you? He doesn't believe it when I say it, but I am okay."

It didn't sound like she was lying—and that realization made tears of relief obscure Randall's vision.

"I believe her," he whispered to David. "She's a tough one, that girl of yours. She's going to be all right."

David nodded slowly, and under his hand Randall could feel his shoulder quiver even more.

"Don't worry," Whitmoore said. "Fred was a doctor before all this."

"Vet," corrected the man, who was now wrapping bandages around Rose's waist to stop the bleeding.

Whitmoore flung out his hand, as if to say: *If it walks like a duck ...*

"The point is: Fred knows what he's doing. She's going to be okay."

"Absolutely," Fred acknowledged. "And the wound actually isn't that bad. The bullet went straight through. But she will need some stitches ... and a bucketload of penicillin."

"Then it's lucky we brought extra."

As he said those words, Whitmoore let his gaze slide over the faces of the crowd. Slowly, so no one could have any doubts that he was talking to them. And so everyone understood it was the medicine from Redwater that was going to save Rose from an otherwise inevitable—and most likely fatal—infection.

The answer came—not in words, but in action,

when Dylan Muller—one of Jack's armed henchmen—walked over to Whitmoore, offered him his hand, and pulled him up.

Once up, Whitmoore nodded at Dylan and patted him on the shoulder. Then he turned towards Randall.

"Can you tell me where I can find Thomas Longhorn? I believe you call him the Mayor."

Randall stared at him, momentarily unable to grasp what he was being asked. Then he shook his head and nodded towards the group where the Mayor was.

Thomas Longhorn no longer had a gun pressed against the back of his head, but he still looked unusually stiff and tense. However, this didn't stop him from strapping on his broad politician's smile and shaking Whitmoore's hand when he was offered it.

And as the two men walked toward the Mayor's caravan, undoubtedly with a strengthened ambition to resolve the conflict together, Randall helped lift Rose onto a stretcher.

On it, she was transported over to the southeastern corner of the corrugated iron building, where the San Hiva camp's doctor—a former school nurse from Swissdale named Ann—had set up a small clinic.

chapter 15

As he sat there on the edge of the bench with his hands folded in his lap and his upper body leaning so far forward that it looked as if he was about to tip over, no one could be in doubt. Guilt and shame were eating up David from the inside.

"How's she doing?"

David shrugged but didn't move his gaze higher than the height of Randall's hip before it fell back to the ground.

"She's still asleep. Did they figure something out?"

"Who?"

"The Mayor and the old guy ... Whitmoore. Isn't that where you went?"

"Well ... yeah, it was," Randall replied, rather amazed that David, amidst all the confusion and panic, had noticed when he got called out from Rose's room an hour ago. "The Redwater camp has invited us to a joint meeting. Our camp and three other camps who also found mass graves. The plan is that we ..."

He realized David wasn't listening anymore, so instead of finishing the sentence, he took a seat next to him on the bench.

For a while, they sat there in silence, next to each other. Randall with his eyes on David, and David with his eyes on nothing.

When he decided the silence had lasted long enough, Randall deliberately took a loud breath and cleared his throat.

"It's not your fault, kid. You know that, don't you? Jack is the guilty one here."

Now, for the first time, David raised his head high enough to meet his gaze.

"I must really look like crap, huh?"

"What do you mean?"

"I don't think I've heard you call me *kid* since ... yeah, well, actually since the very first day we met each other. Tommy still does it sometimes, but never you."

Randall smiled.

"Mm, that's probably true. But that's just because I quickly realized that you're much tougher and more mature than you look."

Randall hesitated a little, then added:

"But sometimes it's okay, you know."

"What's okay?"

"To be a kid. To drop the responsibility and the acting as an adult from time to time. To allow yourself to be ... your actual age, you know. And to make mistakes."

David uttered a despairing sigh and shook his head.

"Not in this new world," he said. "There is no room for mistakes here. If I were still the same dumb teenager you found at that gas station, I wouldn't have survived very long."

"That *dumb teenager*, as you call it, is one of the bravest people I've ever met. All the warning signs you made with the spray cans back then ... Christ, David. If it weren't for that *dumb teenager's* graffiti, the death toll would have been way higher. I don't doubt that for a second."

David raised his index finger as if he were about to counter-argue, but then hesitated and let his hand fall down on his thigh.

"I know you mean well," he said. "You and Tommy saved me, gave me a home, and this last year you two have been ... yeah, kind of like some weird parents to me, I guess."

Behind the grief in his eyes, a fleeting glimpse of something else appeared, and he pulled his lips up in a frosty smile.

"You fight like an old couple too, sometimes, you and Tommy."

Randall smiled and shrugged as if to say: *Siblings. What can you do?*

"But," David said. "You're wrong on this one, though. It *was* my fault. I'm the one who got Rose to go to Jack ... and it was precisely the dumb, impulsive teenager in me who rushed right after her. And if I'm being completely honest, it was most of all the thought that Jack might put his disgusting hands on her again that made me do it. That he would *touch* her, just like he did the other day."

He sighed with exhaustion, put his hands together as if getting ready to pray, and lay his face down in them.

"It was ... fucking jealousy, Randall. That's all. Not heroism because I was afraid that she'd get hurt. I just wanted to smack that son of a bitch right in the face if he put his hands on my girlfriend again."

The pain in David's voice was almost unbearable, and if he had the opportunity, Randall would happily have taken it upon himself. Have carried the cross for him for a while.

But like anyone who cares about someone else the way a parent cares about his child, he had to accept that it simply wasn't an option.

"Who knows?" he said. "You may be right. I mean, both Brent and me saw it was what you said that got Rose to storm in there."

As expected, those words caused David to lift his head from his hands and stare at him, but Randall didn't look back at him. This was hard enough as it was.

"But then again, we both know Rose, don't we?"

he continued. "She'd already made up her mind, and she would have run in there anyway. Whether you gave her an excuse or not."

David uttered a dry, gurgling laugh and nodded.

"Yep, that's Rose, all right."

"Sure is. Rose in a nutshell. There's not a shred of evil in that girl, and if she sees a chance to help others, she grabs it."

David stared at him with eyes that slowly became colder and colder as he started to understand.

"It's *not* Rose's fault," he finally said. Not quite in a snarl, but close. "She had no way of knowing what would happen. That I would follow ..."

He hesitated, swallowed, and once more looked over at Randall, who nodded slowly.

"It's not Rose's fault, no. And it's not yours either. You were pushed into reacting in a situation where there was no time to think. Life is like that sometimes. Hell, it probably won't be the last time you'll be in a situation like that."

David raised one eyebrow and scoffed.

"You're not going to say some shit about sometimes having to take a bullet for your partner in a relationship, are you?

Randall smiled, rolling his eyes.

"Not at all. But if you ask me, it's quite promising for your future together that neither of you hesitated to take responsibility for it. Both of you defended the other without even blinking."

"Maybe."

Although David said no more than this one word, Randall thought he heard a change in the young man's voice. He didn't exactly sound calm, but at least he sounded a bit more balanced than before. Like he wasn't on the verge of throwing himself off a bridge.

And for now, Randall decided, that would have to do.

In a new—but far less tense—period of silence, they sat there, side by side, on the worn wooden bench outside the room where Rose was sleeping.

Ahead of them, the sun had begun to set over the mine crater at the end of the curved dirt road, and the sky had taken on a delicate, orange tinge. Soon, darkness would come, and he would have to leave David here and go home to his biological son.

But it was okay. Because before long, the door behind him would open, and someone would come out here, telling David that Rose had opened her eyes. That she had asked to see him.

And when that happened, David would go in there, take her hand, and tell her he loved her more than anything. Afterward, because it was the one simple truth that mattered, she would do the same.

chapter 16

You fight like an old couple too, sometimes, you and Tommy.

David probably didn't know it, but that comment kept echoing in Randall's head throughout the drive after he left San Hiva and drove back to the farm.

And when he came into the driveway and turned off the car's engine, he had made the final decision: it was time to have a talk with Tommy about poker nights and the people he surrounded himself with. The talk that Randall—halfway consciously, halfway unconsciously—had postponed several times.

Why now? Because Randall had realized something important during his conversation with David. Like David, Tommy had also been robbed of life as he knew it when the civilized world met its demise. Within a fortnight, all of his relationships had disappeared.

And yeah, of course Tommy was reunited with his younger brother, but at that time they hadn't spoken for years. So you couldn't exactly count that as Tommy getting back some of his life.

Considering this, was it really so strange that Tommy was drawn to types like Jack and Dylan? People who, for better or worse, reminded him of the life he had before the world collapsed.

Besides, despite his flaws and his demons, Tommy had never let him down when it mattered. Even after two years of bitter silence between them, he didn't hesitate to jump in the car to pick up Randall when he called him from the phone booth outside of Carol's Diner the day when it all went down.

And he also didn't hesitate to step into the dark corridors of Newcrest Memorial Hospital to help you look for Billy, the thought version of Allie's voice added while Randall opened the car door and got out. *Not even for a second did he—*

His stream of thought was ripped apart when a

shrill, metallic sound cut through the silence of the driveway, causing him to stiffen.

Billy's panic bell.

Without him even registering it, his fingers let go of the car door with a convulsive twitch, and he felt a rush of feverish heat rise up in his chest.

Had the sound come from inside the house, it wouldn't have bothered him. Then it could be innocent things, like Billy dropping one of his comics—or maybe a half-full glass of water—on the floor so he couldn't reach it from his wheelchair.

But the sound of the bell hadn't come from inside the house. It had come from the workshop.

What on earth was Billy doing out there? And what had happened that made him ring the bell for help?

Randall started to walk, first with slow, hesitant steps, then quicker and quicker, as if his feet were trying to catch up with the rising pulse in his ears.

The bell rang again, just as he put his hand on the door handle, triggering another sting of panic and causing him to not only *open* the door but to *tear* it open.

"Randall? Hell, man, what are you doing?"

Randall opened his mouth but couldn't get any words out.

The workshop was actually an extension to the house that their father had built in his day to have a dry place for his old, light brown Buick. But just like his eldest son, Richard Morgan was a bit of a slob, and it didn't take long before the garage was so full of junk that there was no room for the car.

And when Tommy later took over the farm, he turned the garage into a workshop, so he had a place to renovate his Harley Davidson.

The motorcycle was still there, suspended in two thick nylon straps, but he rarely ever touched it. In his defense, it had to be said that the room had changed its function again over the last year.

These days it was the communications room that he and Tommy used to get in touch with other survivors via a shortwave radio they had found in an abandoned electronics store in Gleamsdale.

Tommy and Billy were in front of that radio, right now. Both staring at Randall—with big question marks in their eyes.

"Seriously, Randall," Tommy continued. "What the hell are you doing? You scared the shit out of us, barging in like that."

"Tommy, I ... it was the bell. I heard it and I thought ..."

For a moment, Tommy kept staring at him. Then his gaze slipped onto the bell, which was still in Billy's hand, and he started laughing out loud. So did Billy.

"What's so funny?"

"Sorry," Tommy said, holding his hand up in front of him while he—with obvious strain—stifled his laughter. "It was just your little bumblebee here. He rang the bell as a joke."

Randall looked over at Billy and didn't know whether he should be upset or happy that the boy was sharp enough today to be joking.

"As a joke? You rang your bell, your *panic bell*, as a joke?"

"It's my fault," Tommy said, ruffling Billy's blond hair. "We're playing chess with Mitchell over the radio, and when we lost the first rook, I rang Billy's bell, for fun, you know. And ... well, it kind of became a thing."

He smiled and shrugged embarrassedly.

"So, what you heard before was just the sound of your son losing his queen."

Randall sighed and rubbed a finger over one of his eyebrows while looking over at Billy, who now slowly hung the bell back in place and then gave him an apologetic look.

"It's okay, Billy. I'm just tired. It's been a long day."

Something in his voice must have revealed to Tommy how long the day had actually been, because now he leaned down and pressed the radio's transmitter button.

"I think we're going to call it a night, Mitchell. Randall just got back, and ... yeah, it's also bedtime for Billy soon."

"All right," said a voice in the speaker. "We'll have a rematch another day, Tommy. Say hi from me."

"Of course. You too."

After the brief, metallic click which told him the connection had been severed, there followed a long moment of silence in which Tommy just stood and stared at Randall.

"Did they bring the stuff in from Redwater?" he asked. But what his pitch said was:

What the hell happened?

"They came, yes. But there were some ... complications."

As he spoke, Randall walked over to the right side of the room, where a stack of old garden chairs was standing against the wall. He took one of these chairs and dragged it with him all the way over to Billy, where he placed it on the floor next to the wheelchair and let himself fall into it.

"Complications? What does that mean?"

"Your buddy, Jack, tried to start ... yeah, what should we call it? A riot? A civil war?"

"Oh, that dumb fuck."

"Yep. But the worst thing is that he had actually managed to get a pretty big group behind him."

Tommy nodded and didn't look the slightest bit surprised.

"People are afraid, and when they are, it's easy for someone like Jack to become a mouthpiece for them."

"A *megaphone* would probably be a more fitting term," Randall said and rolled his eyes.

"But you got away alive?"

"Barely, yes."

"What's that supposed to mean?"

"We'll talk about that one later."

Tommy squinted, and Randall answered him by shaking his head and then nodding discreetly towards Billy.

"Later," Tommy confirmed. "But you did get the delivery, right?"

"We did. And once the other stuff had been sorted out, the Mayor and a guy named Whitmoore held a meeting that went pretty well. Turns out that Redwater has invited San Hiva and three other camps, who also found mass graves, to a large joint meeting. They offered to have it in the big football stadium over there, so there's room for all of those who want to come. The idea is that every camp will have an influence on how we handle the whole reconstruction thing, now that ..."

"Now that the enemy has given up overnight

and voluntarily laid down to die," Tommy concluded for him, with sarcasm in his voice that couldn't be missed. "*After* they've wiped out ninety percent of us without breaking a sweat, mind you."

Part of Randall was annoyed by the comment because he wanted to cling to the hope that the suffering might be over. That the invisible enemy had simply disappeared, suddenly and relatively undramatically, like the aliens in Orwell's *War of the Worlds*, who in the end were defeated by Earth's diseases to which they were not immune.

But another part of Randall—the one in which a good deal of paranoia had been cultivated after the terrible events he had lived through the year before—had no trouble seeing Tommy's logic.

"Are you planning on going?"

Tommy's question—and the concern in his voice—left Randall speechless for a moment. For he suddenly realized that the answer would determine which of the two feelings dueling inside of him—*hope* or *fear*—would be allowed to win. And that it was an *either-or* choice. That he'd have to go all-in and remain on whichever side he chose.

"I ... yeah, I suppose I am," he said—and then again, this time louder and without wavering: "Yes, I'm going. If we really want a chance to rebuild and get back to something resembling a normal life, this has to be our best bet."

"A pipe dream," Tommy said. "Things will *never* get back to being the way they were before."

"Perhaps not, but I owe it to Billy to try. Living in a world where no one trusts each other, and people get shot just for trying to ... We have to be better than that. Hell, we *are* better than that! And before I demand trust from others, I have to show it myself. So yes, I'm going to that meeting. *We* are going to that meeting."

He heard it in his own voice when it slid off track and broke, and he saw in Tommy's eyes that it hadn't slipped his attention either.

"What the hell happened out there today, Randall?"

Randall let his eyes fall to the floor and nodded slowly. Then he got up from the chair and put his hand on top of Billy's.

"Tommy and I are going outside for a minute,

but I'll be back soon, and then you're going to bed, okay?"

Billy looked up at him and accepted the deal with a smile.

When they had gotten out in the driveway and closed the door to the workshop behind them, Randall stood still for a moment, pulling a few breaths of the cool evening air into his lungs. Only after doing that did he feel ready to meet his older brother's gaze.

"I didn't want to say anything in front of Billy," he said. "I'll tell him later. It's Rose. She tried to calm Jack down, but it went wrong, and ... she got hit."

"Got hit? Like as in shot?"

"She's okay," Randall said quickly. "But yes, Jack hit her. A bullet, just above the hip bone. Fortunately, it went right through."

"Holy shit, man. But you say she's okay? You're sure about that?"

"She's okay. It was a lucky shot, if you can put it like that. The biggest danger is the risk of infection, but fortunately the people from Redwater had plenty of antibiotics in their truck."

"Good," Tommy said. "That's good. What about David? Is he okay?"

"He will be. Right now, he's struggling with guilt because he thinks it was something he said that made her go in there."

"Damn, man. Can you imagine if he'd lost her? It's not like he has that much else. And then right now, when they've only just moved in together."

In a glimpse, the thought Randall had sat with in the car on the way home resurfaced, and he once more felt a sting of guilt for only now having realized how many similarities there were between Tommy and David's stories.

"Tommy, I've been thinking. Maybe it's time for you and me to have a chat about ... well, everything, I guess. How things are going, you know. Not an argument. No pointing fingers. Just a relaxed talk between two brothers. Maybe we could even put a worm on a hook and go down to Dad's old place by the creek?"

For what felt like an eternity, Tommy's gray eyes stared at him with an expression Randall couldn't decipher. It could be confusion; it could be defiance ... but it could also be relief.

"That ... sounds like a good plan," he finally said. "I'd like that."

"Perfect, we'll do that then," Randall replied, giving him an awkward jab on the shoulder that they both knew was a substitute for the hug they weren't quite ready to give each other yet.

Just as they both knew that the conversation had reached its natural end and only needed for one of them to make it official.

Tommy took the initiative, rubbing his shoulders and saying:

"Well, I think I'm going to pop into the living room and throw a few logs in the stove. It's too goddamn cold to stay out here."

As if to agree with Tommy by giving a physical demonstration of how cold it actually was, Randall puffed out into the air and studied his own breath, which could now be seen clearly as a cloud of white. Then he nodded.

"Yeah, I also need to get back to Billy. We'll be there in a minute."

chapter 17

"Sorry about that, Billy," Randall said as he came back into the workshop. "Tommy and I had something we needed to talk about."

Billy moved his hand sideways through the air as if waving away a fly, and at the same time uttered a little snorting sound. His way of saying: *Don't think about it.*

"It looked like you were having fun with Tommy."

"Mistell," Billy said—that was his version of Mitchell—pointing to the radio. "Chess."

"Yeah, I see that. Was Mitchell good at it?"

Billy made big eyes and nodded his head up and down with an eagerness that made Randall smile.

"Oh, really? That good?"

Billy nodded again.

"You know, I can believe that," Randall said as he walked around back and grabbed the wheelchair's handles. "Mitchell could've been one of those guys who played chess at the little stone tables in the parks before."

He started pushing the chair, then hesitated.

"I missed you today, Billy ... a lot. But I'm glad you had such a good time with Tommy at home."

Billy didn't say anything, but he leaned to the side of the seat, twisted his upper body, and raised his hand, grazing Randall's elbow.

On most days, Randall wouldn't have read any particularly deep motives into such a gesture. But today it made his throat close up, because it really felt as if that little motion was Billy telling him that everything was going to be all right.

When they got to the door, Randall let go of one of the handles, reached out his hand, and turned off the light switch, leaving the workshop in darkness.

Except it wasn't completely dark. Down at the opposite end of the room there were three small, glowing balls of light. Two orange-colored bulbs and one green.

Didn't Tommy turn off the radio? I could have sworn that he did.

"Just a second, Billy," he said, flicking the light switch on the wall back on. "I have to turn off the radio."

He let go of the wheelchair, went to the old desk where the radio was placed, and pushed the tiny lever down, so it jumped from *On* to *Off*.

The speaker buzzed for a second or two, and then the lights in the bulbs started to die out. First the green one, then the first of the orange ones, then—

Something tipped over somewhere behind him and hit the concrete floor with a loud clang, making him jump.

The first thing he saw as he turned around was Billy holding his hands up apologetically in front of himself. The next was the ugly-ass coat stand (four flimsy metal legs with the skull of a bull sitting on top) that Tommy had bought at a flea market long ago. It was lying on the floor now because Billy had accidentally bumped into it with his wheelchair.

"It's okay, hon. I'll get it."

He walked over there, picked up the coat stand, and then bent down to pick up the things that had hung on it. One of them was Tommy's backpack and the other was a worn, dark gray motorcycle jacket.

Randall never made it to the jacket, though, because when he grabbed the backpack, he saw that something had fallen out of it. A small, semitransparent plastic bag.

"What the hell is that, Tommy?" he muttered through his teeth as he gently grabbed its corner and lifted it up so he could study its contents.

And when he realized that there could be no explanation other than the one which had been his first impulse at the sight of the white powder, the question became a hot, burning indictment.

One he didn't hesitate to run out the workshop door to direct at his brother.

chapter 18

The bag hit Tommy right smack in the middle of his face, making him drop both the paper and the tobacco he was about to roll into it out on the coffee table. With no pause, the next attack followed; a volley of words sent out with just as much strength:

"WHAT THE HELL IS THIS, TOMMY?"

Tommy held his hands out to the sides and stared uncomprehendingly down at his sweater, which was now strewn with finely cut tobacco. From there, his gaze went down to the bag with the white powder and finally up to his brother's face.

"Randall ... what the hell?"

"You looked after Billy!" Randall sneered, as if it were the indisputable, universal, and definitive explanation to anything Tommy could think to ask.

In a way, it was.

"Seriously, Randall. I really don't know what—"

"No! Hell no, Tommy. Don't even *think* about giving me some farfetched story. What is it? Flour? Icing sugar? You were looking after my fucking son! You agreed to take care of him, and then I find this kind of ... shit in your bag."

At the last three words—*in your bag*—Tommy tilted his head and squinted his eyes. He was good. It almost looked real. But of course, he also had years of experience with playing dumb every time their mom found drugs and booze in his room.

"How long?"

"What do you mean?"

The question—and the stupid, confused fish face Tommy gave along with his answer—got the blood boiling in Randall's veins. He felt like grabbing Tommy's neck hair, holding his head tight, and shaking the bag in front of his nose like he was a dog that had gnawed a shoe to pieces.

"Yeah, what the hell do you *think* I mean? How long have you been snorting this shit? Or whatever it is you do with it."

"I haven't snorted anything," Tommy said,

annoyingly calmly. "Not that, and not anything else."

"I found it in *your* bag."

"I don't know what to say to that. It's not mine ... and why were you going through my stuff, by the way?"

"I wasn't. It fell down. Stop changing the subject."

Tommy raised one eyebrow.

"Are you hearing yourself?"

"Honestly, Tommy? After all the shit we've been through together, you choose to lie to me now?"

"I'm not lying. Why would I—"

"Because you are *you*. Because that's what you do!"

Without letting his eyes stray from his brother, Tommy picked up the bag from the couch where it had landed.

For a second, Randall thought he was going to throw it back in his face. But Tommy didn't throw the bag with the white powder. Instead, he opened it, raised it up to his nose and nodded.

"It is some kind of drug," he said, looking up.

"But it's not mine. I've been clean for years, Randall. Hell, you know that."

"I only know what I see," Randall snarled. "And what I see is that you've been away more and more often from home, hanging out with the likes of Jack and Dylan ... and that you've started drinking again."

"If this is about Jack and me having a few beers before that meeting ..."

"Damn it, Tommy! Listen for once! I don't give a rat's ass that you got drunk at that meeting. It was immature and stupid, yes ... but nothing more."

He pointed in the direction of the bag with a finger that quivered so much it looked as if he were trying to make its contents explode by the sheer power of thought.

"But this, Tommy. This, when you're responsible for Billy, is simply ..."

Even now, in a state of anger that felt so red-hot that his body could barely contain it, Randall was aware of the weight of the word on the tip of his tongue. Aware of its caliber.

But he said it anyway.

"Unforgivable, Tommy. That's what it is. Fucking *unforgivable*."

Tommy took a deep breath and bit his lower lip. *Chewed* it. Above his left eyebrow, the contours of a vein appeared. Like a small, thick earthworm twisting slowly under the skin of his temple.

"It's not my bag," he said. "It's *not* my bag!"

Although they were the exact same words that came out of his mouth twice in a row, it sounded like two completely different sentences with completely different messages. The first one came out as an uncomprehending whisper, a sort of: *I refuse to believe this*, whereas the ensuing, far louder and more snarling, seemed to carry a meaning along the lines of: *Who the fuck do you think you are*?

For a moment, he left the words hanging in the air while he himself did nothing but stare at Randall. It was as if he expected that such a clear answer would trigger an immediate apology. After all, he had said it *twice*.

It didn't work, so he changed his strategy. He got up from the couch, threw the bag to the floor and grabbed the back of his head in frustration.

"Unforgivable? Randall, come on, man. Think it through. Why would I, after so many years without drugs, start that shit again?"

Randall shrugged—and then it came to him. The perfect, hurtful remark that he wouldn't have dreamed of saying had his sense of empathy not been swallowed up in a sea of anger.

"I gave up trying to understand why you do the things you do a long time ago, Tommy ... just like Mom did."

That was below the belt, Randall. Apologize to him.

His inner version of Allie was right. Using their mother like that *was* below the belt, no doubt about it. Because Rita Morgan was effectively the only person in the family who didn't turn her back on Tommy after the stunt he pulled at their dad's funeral. Even though she was the one his drunken monologue hit hardest as it had forever put a stain on her last goodbye to her husband. Yet she had never wavered in her love for Tommy and never abandoned him.

The effect of the words was almost downright creepy to observe on Tommy's face. Like the prize labels of a wheel of fortune, a series of different emotions flashed by in it until the wheel's needle stopped at a dark, clenched facial expression.

"It must be nice being you," he said—and before Randall had the chance to ask what he meant, he continued with a thick, sarcastic undertone in his voice: "Randall Morgan. The great writer who never has any trouble finding just the right words. The ones that really hit home. But you know what, Randall? I don't have to put up with this shit because it's not my bag, and it's not my drugs. So fuck you, fuck your accusations ... and fuck your oh-so-well-chosen words!"

He emphasized his last two words by kicking, first the edge of the couch, then the coffee table, making it slide sideways. Then he strode over to the bookcase, grabbed his car keys from the little basket they were in, and continued out into the hallway.

Randall stood still for a moment, torn between the urge to run after his brother or scream at him. But before he could do either, he heard the sound of a door being ripped open and slammed shut, followed by a short pause and then the sound of spinning wheels.

Following that—leaving aside the chaotic vortex of thoughts in his head—everything fell quiet in the living room.

part 4

REDWATER

"There's a bullet in my barrel,

but I don't know who it's for.

Through the windows to your soul

it's not you I see no more."

— O. E. *Geralt*, In Other Words.

chapter 19

Two days after the fight with his brother, Randall got up before sunrise and spent fifteen minutes on the back terrace with a cup of coffee in his hand and a plan to spend the day taking a trip to the San Hiva camp forming in his head.

The purpose of the trip was two-sided. On the one hand, Randall wanted to visit Rose to see how she was, and on the other hand he would like to ask his older brother's buddies if any of them had heard from him. Tommy hadn't returned home yet after the argument, nor had he shown signs of life in any other way, and this worried Randall a bit.

After taking the last sip of his coffee, he got up from the bench and went into the kitchen, where he prepared breakfast. Then he woke up Billy and let him in on the plan.

An hour later, the boy's wheelchair was folded up in the trunk of Randall's old Ford, and they were headed for San Hiva.

When they arrived at the camp, they only just managed to park the car before David came running over to them.

"Randall!"

He shouted his name with a strange enthusiasm. As if it were a word in a difficult crossword puzzle, and he had just figured it out.

"You have to help me," he continued, slightly out of breath from running. "You can talk to her. She'll listen to you."

Randall opened the door and got out of the car. Then he stared at David, assessed him—and came to the conclusion that there was nothing seriously wrong.

"I take it we're talking about Rose. What's up with her?"

"She's stubborn," David said, after which he bent down and waved at Billy in the passenger seat. "Hey there, Billy!"

The boy waved back at him and then drew two

small circles in the air while looking at Randall.

Randall nodded and went around to the trunk of the car.

"I'm afraid you're going to have to give me a little more to go on than that, David. Rose being stubborn isn't exactly a secret. And give me a hand with this, will you?"

David grabbed one of the crossbars of the folded wheelchair, tried pulling it, and then moved his hand further up.

"Here?"

"I think so. Try tilting it a ... yep, that did it. Thanks."

"Sure. She wants to go on Friday. *That's* why she's stubborn."

"On Friday ... to Redwater?"

David nodded.

"Is she in a condition to do that?"

David wrinkled his nose and tilted his head slightly. Not quite a no, but not a yes either.

Randall nodded, then pretended that it required his full attention to fold out the wheelchair and lift Billy into it.

In reality, he could probably do both things with his eyes closed and one hand tied behind his back by now, but he wasn't going to side with David without at least seeing Rose first.

Maybe something in his performance revealed this to David. In any case, the young man changed the subject as he waved them over toward his new home.

"You still haven't heard anything from him?"

"Tommy? Nope, nothing."

"You must have really gone at it. It's not like him to stay away that long."

"Yeah, I guess the waves rolled pretty high, but ... what? Did I say something funny?"

David, who apparently didn't even realize that his lips had pulled up in a smile, immediately wiped it off.

"No, not funny, really. I just got a flashback to when I'd just met you guys. I hadn't been with you very long, and the two of you had a little fight. I was sitting in the back seat, and I remember you turning around afterward, saying the same thing to me. That the waves tend to roll high when you and

Tommy are together."

"Oh, really?"

"Yeah, I remember it very clearly because ... well, it was at that exact moment I decided to trust you guys."

Randall was on the verge of asking why, but then he realized that the answer was obvious. Back then, David, a high school student, had been all alone for more than a week in a world where everyone seemed to have lost their minds. Bearing that in mind, witnessing a family argument must have felt pretty ... well, normal. Human, even.

What he had expected to see when they opened the door to the trailer, Randall didn't quite know. Perhaps a pale, weakened Rose under the duvet with a cup of tea in her hand or a pale, weakened Rose in an armchair with an IV-drip in her arm.

Whatever he expected to see, it was certainly not this. An upright, humming Rose who was warming a can of chili con carne over a gas burner. A Rose whose only visible sign of involvement in a shooting was the white bandage that could occasionally be glimpsed under the edge of her T-shirt when she raised her arm.

"Hey, Randall," she exclaimed. "Where's ... oh, there you are, Billy. I couldn't see you behind the door."

"Careful with the wound, babe," David said as Rose walked over and bent down to give Billy a kiss on the cheek. Rose just rolled her eyes at him and winked at Billy, then held her hands up in front of him with five fingers outstretched on one hand and two on the other.

"Seven stitches, Billy," she boasted, turning sideways so she could show where on her hip they were placed. "Front *and* back. Isn't that cool? Like a cowboy. Or Rambo."

Billy smiled at her and nodded with approval, even though Randall strongly doubted that the boy had the faintest idea who John Rambo was.

"You look better than I expected."

"Why, thank you, Randall," Rose said, sending David a *what did I tell you*? look. "I'm glad someone sees it."

"It's one thing to prance around here at home," David protested. "It's another to stand on a football field with tons of other people who push and shove and... j-jostle."

"Jostle?" Rose repeated with a wry smile.

"What? It's a word."

"Tons of other people?" Randall repeated. "Does that mean there is a lot of support?"

For a moment, David stared at him as if it were the most foolish question he'd heard in his life. Then he shook his head.

"Oh, yeah, you haven't been here. But yeah, the support has been overwhelming. And it's not only from the camps who also found mass graves. Almost all the camps San Hiva has had radio contact with have agreed to come. And here in camp as well. The vast majority have decided to go."

On David's lips, a small, gleeful smile appeared.

"Ironically, I think it was Jack's ... rebellion that convinced most of them. Fucking idiot."

"Don't, babe," Rose said. "He was scared, and he wasn't alone in it. He's taking his punishment, too, isn't he? Besides, he apologized to us."

David pretended not to hear her, and simply continued to speak to Randall.

"After he shot Rose, everyone could easily see what would have happened if we hadn't gotten those antibiotics from Redwater. And I think that convinced the ones in doubt."

Randall instinctively looked over at Rose, who immediately read the question in his eyes and shook her head.

"No infection."

"Not yet," David saw his chance to interject. "But if she doesn't get enough rest and take care of the wound, that could easily change."

"David, come on. I've *made* my decision. And I'm glad you worry about me, but I've also explained to you why I want to go. Why I *have* to go. Trust works both ways, so I'm not planning on hiding here at home when all the others are going."

David sent Randall a look that was an obvious request for support ... but Randall found himself unable to give it. Because he understood what Rose meant when she said that trust had to work both ways. If you boiled it down to the essence, it was more or less what he had argued the other day when he explained to Tommy why they ought to go.

He shook his head slowly, and David closed his eyes. Kept them closed for a while, grinding his teeth. Then he sighed and opened them again.

"We'll stay off the field. Away from the crowd."

Rose nodded and put on a gentle smile.

"Of course. And I'll be careful."

"We can go together," Randall interjected. "I'm not going to drag Billy into the middle either, with his wheelchair and stuff."

David gave him a *well, it's better than nothing, I guess* nod and then walked over to the gas burner, where he grabbed the spoon and started stirring what was in the pan.

Behind his back, Rose sent a wordless message to Randall, who immediately nodded and said:

"What do you say, Billy? Why don't we take a walk around camp? Then we can ask if anyone has seen Tommy?"

Billy answered him with a thumbs-up, and to Randall's surprise, it actually seemed as if the boy was fully aware that the suggestion was just an excuse for giving Rose and David a bit of privacy.

The short walk ended up being a longer affair. Partly because Billy insisted on going all the way up the curved dirt road behind the camp so he could see the coal crater, and partly because Randall stopped every time they met others to ask if any of them had seen Tommy around.

No one had.

chapter 20

When, a few hours later, he left the main road and turned onto the dirt road leading to the driveway, there was a brief moment when Randall thought his brother had finally returned home.

But he was disappointed. Badly disappointed.

In all fairness, the military truck had some similarities to Tommy's truck, especially when the green cover was peeled off as it was now. But as soon as he spotted the white star on the side of the vehicle, any doubt was gone.

"Fucking shit," he muttered—ignoring the shocked look Billy sent him from the passenger seat. Sometimes swear words were justified, and if the two people standing next to the military vehicle in the driveway were the ones the Mayor had warned him about, then this was definitely one of those situations.

He lifted his foot from the accelerator and let the car roll slowly across the gravel as he tried to figure out the best strategy for dealing with his unexpected guests.

Turning back was, of course, an option, but if they had bothered to find their way out here to Tommy's farm, they would undoubtedly just come back another day.

So no, he might as well grab the bull by the horns and give them a clear message from the start. Make them understand that he would rather see the whole world burn than voluntarily hand his son over to strangers. Especially strangers who wore uniforms, just as the police officers had done.

"Billy, once we get into the driveway, I'd like you to stay in the car while I talk to our guests. Can you do that?"

Billy looked at him and answered with a nod and a shrug. He then turned his attention to the trees on the right side of the car, probably to spot birds, which was one of the few interests he had retained from before.

While he did that, Randall reached out his hand, opened the glove compartment and—as discreetly as possible—pulled out his Smith & Wesson. He hoped he wouldn't need it, but he preferred to be on the safe side.

Once he had entered the driveway, he parked all the way over on the opposite side. Then he got out and walked, quickly, toward the guests, thus making the distance between them and Billy as wide as possible.

One was a woman. He hadn't been able to see that from a distance. She was pretty, too. At least he would have thought so under normal circumstances, even if he at this moment felt a greater urge to tell her to go to hell than to stare deep into her hazel brown eyes.

Her partner was a man, and he, on the other hand, *wasn't* very good-looking. In fact, he came close to being the woman's exact opposite. Where her golden hair hung in elegant, curvy tresses, framing and complimenting her face, his looked like something that had been both cut and combed using only a rusty machete.

He was, however, rather intimidating, and that also had its value in the world they lived in now.

But it was the woman who called the shots. That was the clear feeling Randall got as they walked toward him. And indeed, she was the one to speak first.

"Randall Morgan?"

"That's what it says on my birth certificate. What can I do for you?"

"My name is Helen Walker, and this is Robert Faulkner. We come from ARL in Maryland, where I worked as a researcher until ... well, I suppose I don't have to explain that part."

She pulled her lips up in a friendly smile, which Randall, despite his reluctance, had to make an effort not to return.

"Nah, I think I can imagine," he replied, after which he—with what he hoped was an impatient *no time for bullshit* tone in his voice—repeated his question. "What was it I can do for you?"

"We ... um, we've been looking for you for a while, actually. Or, for the *two of you*, I should probably say, because it's kind of your son who's primarily caught our interest. Is that him?"

As she asked the question, she looked over at Billy in the car. So did Randall—and he made sure to turn sideways while doing it so she couldn't avoid seeing the gun sticking out from the jeans under his jacket.

"That's my son, yes."

"And is it true what the rumors say?"

"How should I know what rumors you hear?"

For a split second, the woman looked completely startled, but just as quickly she got herself back on track.

"That he was one of the abducted children," she said. "That you found him in one of the hospitals and freed him *after* he was ... treated. *That* is what the rumors say."

Treated? Is that what you call it when you pump little kids full of tadpoles?

"You shouldn't believe everything you hear," Randall said, shrugging his shoulders indifferently.

"You're preaching to the choir," the woman replied, pointing to the laminated sign on her chest, which, in addition to her name, also had the title *SENIOR RESEARCHER* written on it. "That could be my motto. But you know what I still kind of ... *believe*?"

"What?"

"I believe you're shying away from my question."

"Listen," Randall said. "Maybe I've just had a really long day and maybe I then came home to a couple of uninvited guests in my driveway who want to speak to my son because they've heard some absurd rumors."

That was half the truth. He *had* had a long day, and he *was* tired. But first and foremost, he was trying to ruffle her feathers. To provoke a reaction that would give him an excuse to throw them out the gate.

But the woman was irritatingly calm and just left his words hanging like an annoying insect in the air until they had lost all their power.

"If I've offended you, Mr. Morgan, it certainly wasn't my intention," she said. "I understand that it must be confusing, us showing up out of the blue.

And in the light of that, it might be tempting to hold back some information because you think it's best for your child. That would be a natural reaction from a parent, wouldn't it? In fact, I probably would have done something similar in your shoes."

This confession—whether it was the actual truth or just some rhetorical trick—pulled the rug out from under Randall, and he found himself unable to answer.

"But that being said," she continued. "I'd like for you to consider this: *if* your son ... *if* Billy actually was in a hospital, and *if* he survived being freed from his IV, then he's the only one. No other child has survived it. The others, they ... they went straight into a coma and died after a very short time. All of them. Except Billy."

"What is it you want?" Randall asked—but not entirely with the cold cynicism he wanted to uphold. Because something in the woman's eyes had changed when she said that the children went into comas and died. Something slid over them—something that looked like sincere grief—and it had affected him.

"We want to see if we can figure out what makes Billy so special. If we had the chance to examine him, the knowledge that gives us might enable us to save others."

Those were strong words, and for a second Randall felt torn. But it was no more than a second, because right after, a picture—a halfway unconscious Billy sitting with a plastic hose in his arm, as he had done in the auditorium at Newcrest Memorial Hospital—appeared in his mind.

Suddenly it was no problem to find the cynicism again.

"Examine him? As in *experiment* on him?"

"No, not like that at all, Mr. Morgan. You misinterpret me. I assure you that—"

"Mr. Morgan," Randall snidely repeated. "It's ironic. Do you know when the last time was someone called me Mr. Morgan?"

"Uh ... no?"

"It was just over a year ago when I met a police officer. He also called me Mr. Morgan, and he also assured me that I could trust him ... right before he tried to hang me from a lamppost."

The woman backed up a step, and it dawned on Randall that his hand had moved down to the gun in his jeans without him noticing.

After a brief reflection, however, he decided to leave it there.

"I'm very sorry that I'm unable to help you," he said. "But as I said, you have to be careful about believing everything you hear... and now I think it's high time I got back to my son. So, if there is nothing else ...?"

Behind the woman, her partner stepped forward, but she stopped him with a raised hand. She then put her other hand in her pocket, pulled out a small card, and reached it over to Randall.

"My business card," she said. "Just in case."

Randall hesitated, but then eventually took the card, and as soon as he had done so, the woman nodded as if to say: *Well, then that's in order*. Then she turned toward her colleague and waved for him to come along with her.

Randall remained in place as they got into the truck and started driving. Only when it was all the way out of the driveway did he take his eyes off it and move them down to the business card in his hand.

HELEN WALKER

SENIOR RESEARCHER; BIOCHEMISTRY A2

ARL RESEARCH CENTER

2100 RAVEN ROAD

ADELPHI, MARYLAND

chapter 21

After witnessing the fall of the orderly world first-hand, Randall didn't really feel there was anything left that was capable of shocking him.

Turned out he was wrong.

The Redwater football stadium was far from being the largest sports arena he had seen in his life, and like most other buildings, it was visibly marked by the long period of time when no one had visited or maintained it.

But as it stood there, a large, oval concrete building in pale white and orange colors, in stark contrast with the dark gray sky above, the arena seemed enormous, almost majestic.

That was part of what made Randall open his eyes wide and exchange a glance with David in the passenger seat as they left the main road and got the first glimpse of their destination.

But what shocked him most wasn't the Redwater football stadium itself. It was the number of cars that were parked outside of it.

It's like a freaking rock concert, he thought, and while he obviously knew that was an exaggeration, the sensation was true enough. He felt a kind of awe at the sight of the many cars—and at the thought that they had actually been driven here by people like themselves.

Other survivors.

"Wow!" said Rose, who apparently had just discovered the cars. "Look at that, Billy! Look how many showed up!"

In the rearview mirror, Randall watched his son lean in over Rose and then pull his mouth up in a smile. For a moment, it rubbed off on himself, but then he had another thought that put a damper on it:

Did Billy—who used to collect baseball cards—have the faintest idea what kind of building he was staring at? Was there enough access to his brain's memory center for him to remember that his father had once taken him to watch the Pirates of Pittsburgh play in a similar building?

He considered asking but found that he was afraid of the answer. Therefore, he instead pushed the thought aside and tried to focus on all the positive things this day represented. That it could potentially be the start of rebuilding society.

That idea was intoxicating ... but it also felt utopian and fragile.

Five minutes later, when he turned into the section of the parking area which, according to the signs, was called B3, the idea of the rock concert returned to Randall.

For reasons he couldn't quite identify, it was festival guests he saw when he looked at the many people sitting in small groups out there. Like the ones he had seen countless times on television when they ran old clips from Woodstock.

Maybe it was the way they sat; some on the trunks of cars, some in circles on the ground—some even with a ukulele- or guitar-playing member.

It could also be the simple fact that there were

some similarities between the ungroomed *I've spent three days at a festival without a single shower* look and the new standard of personal hygiene that the end of times had set for most people.

Whatever it was, one thing was clear: what he saw out there on the other side of the windshield was hope. Hope for a better world—perhaps not unlike what the participants at Woodstock had felt back then.

They found a parking spot between an old Mustang and a van whose sides were adorned with advertisements for a hardware store in Patton.

David was the first to get out, and after stretching his legs for a moment, he opened the back door for Rose and Billy while Randall got the wheelchair from the trunk.

"I think we should have brought an umbrella," Rose said after joining them outside.

Randall pulled some air in through his nose and looked up. The air was cold and damp, and in the sky a large cluster of dark clouds moving their way had apparently decided that traveling in a flock was more fun. Should only a few more of the same kind choose to join the team up there, Rose would undoubtedly be right.

The walk across the parking lot led them past several of the groups Randall had seen on the way in, and as a kind of ironic extension of the Woodstock image, the air around some of them carried the unmistakable smell of marijuana.

Of the four visible entrances on this side of the stadium, only one was in use, while the other three were blocked off. However, the barriers themselves gave the impression of being something the Redwater group had put up just for show, given that they consisted of wooden pallets tied together with something that looked like nylon rope.

The open entrance was manned, but contrary to what Randall had expected, none of the guards carried weapons. Not visibly, at least.

Whether he found that observation reassuring or not, he couldn't quite decide.

Like the other three entrances, the open one had a wide staircase leading up to a large arch-shaped hallway, which had to be the passage into the arena itself.

On the stairs was a queue of twelve to fifteen people, and upon taking their place at the end of it, Rose raised her forearm and said:

"Look. Goosebumps."

"Yeah, I know. It's like ... being back, you know," David replied with a strangely profound, almost philosophical sound in his voice.

He didn't elaborate on what he meant, but it wasn't necessary. Randall understood that it was the sight of so many people gathered in one place.

That—and then the feeling of being a part of something organized ... which, mind you, didn't involve hanging innocent people from lampposts.

"How many do you think there are?"

Before Randall and David were ready to give their estimates, they were beaten to it by a woman in a worn yellow raincoat, who, along with two middle-aged men, stood in front of them in the line.

"I've heard there's going to be more than *a thousand*," she said, nodding emphatically.

The way she accentuated the words *a thousand* almost made Randall burst into laughter. She sounded like a child telling her friends in kindergarten that octopuses have *nine* brains.

This didn't mean, though, that the rumor couldn't be true. Because when he looked at the number of people out here—and then took into account that a lot had probably been let through the gates already—a thousand wasn't a completely wild guess.

The line moved, and Randall did his best to follow its rhythm, although the tall steps of the staircase weren't exactly made for wheelchairs.

However, with a little help from David, it worked out, and before long, all four of them stood at the top of the stairs, looking out over the football field on the inside of the arena.

In all honesty, Randall wasn't entirely sure he would have been able to see that it was a football field had it not been framed by the oval, Colosseum-like building. Because what lay under the open roof, surrounded by rows and rows of blue, sun-bleached seats, wasn't a green, clean-cut grass carpet with white painted zone lines.

It was a yellowish, overgrown sea of dried grass.

"Number, names, and camp?" asked the man at the door—a short man in his forties with a dark mustache of the type Randall's ex-wife would have called a *slug*. And since the man never really looked up from his notepad—and also wore a military green cap, the visor of which covered most of his face—this bushy mustache was really the only distinguishable feature of his face.

"We are four in total. Two from San Hiva and two from ... well, it's not a camp, per se, but East Alin."

"And names?"

"Randall and Billy Morgan. We're the ones from East Alin."

The doorman jotted it down on his pad, then lifted the pen and turned it so its lid pointed toward Rose.

"Rose Lavine. San Hiva."

"And you?"

"David Pearson. San Hiva, too. We ... um, we live together."

It was only when Rose stroked him lovingly on his arm and smiled at him that David realized that this final detail—the fact that he and Rose lived together—was completely irrelevant to the doorman, and he became visibly embarrassed.

The doorman didn't comment on it, though. He just pointed the pen once more, this time in the direction of the football field. Randall did, however, notice the hint of a smile under the slug as they walked past him and continued through the arch-shaped passage.

Where the passage ended, a new stairway began, this one running all the way down to the overgrown football field, while giving access to the stands on both sides.

"What are you looking for?" Rose asked.

"A ramp," Randall replied. "It's too narrow between the seats for Billy's wheelchair. But there's got to be a space made for disabled people in a place like this, right?"

You're asking that after a year and a half with a son in a wheelchair? Allie scoffed in his thoughts, and he caught himself answering her:

Now, we haven't exactly been to a lot of concerts and sports games lately, have we, Allison? The world ended, remember?

"Oh crap, I found it," David sighed, pointing up to a platform that hung some distance above the rows of seats on one side—and which could indeed be accessed via a ramp.

"Why are you moaning like that?" Rose asked.

David rubbed his neck and grimaced—something Randall had seen him do in exactly the same way before. Specifically, on the free-floating walkway that connected two of the buildings at Newcrest Memorial Hospital.

"He doesn't like heights."

Rose looked at David, who nodded.

"You never told me that."

He shrugged.

"Never came up, I guess. It's not like we've had plans to visit the Space Needle or anything. Then I would have mentioned it."

Rose looked at him with eyes that were little more than two narrow crevices.

"And maybe it's not something I'm too proud of either," he added reluctantly. "It's not very macho, not being able to clean a gutter without getting dizzy."

"It's okay," Rose said. "Randall can just take Billy up there, and then we can—"

"No. The deal was that you weren't gonna get pushed around down here. You're going up there."

"And what about you?"

"I'll ... try to go up there, and if I can't, I'll just find a seat right below."

For a moment, Rose looked as if she was going to insist, but then—perhaps to avoid drilling deeper into a subject that was obviously sensitive to her boyfriend—she just shrugged and smiled.

"Fine with me. Just don't bail on me."

"Wouldn't dream of it."

As they walked over to the platform, Randall once more let his gaze slide toward the center of the football field, where an ever-growing group of people circled an improvised stage. This too was made with the Redwater camp's favorite material, stacked wooden pallets, as the mainstay.

Up on the stage, three people were debating something. One of them was James Whitmoore, Randall was pretty sure of that, even though the suede jacket had been replaced with a dark gray winter coat.

It made sense, Randall concluded. If you needed to find someone with the charisma and authority to speak on a day like this, Whitmoore was a good choice. He had proven that he had the rhetoric skills of a good leader.

"Looks like it's time for the bumblebee to fly a bit," David said as they reached the ramp that would take them to the platform.

"What do you mean?"

Instead of answering Randall's question with words, David pointed down at the barrier chain that hung between the half walls on either side of the ramp, bolted to one side and attached to a metal ring on the other. With a padlock, of course.

"A ramp for the disabled that takes three full-grown people to get a wheelchair user up on," Randall said as he bent down and lifted Billy out of his wheelchair. "That has got to be the definition of irony."

He waited until David had gotten the wheelchair lifted past the chain, and then handed Billy over to him. Afterward, he crawled over it himself.

Somewhere between fifteen and twenty steps. That was as far as David managed to walk up the steep ramp before Randall noticed his hand sliding out to seek the support of the half-wall.

After another ten or fifteen steps, that hand had begun to shake, and shortly thereafter, the inevitable happened: David stopped.

"Yep. That's about as far as I go."

Rose stared at him, clearly surprised at how strong his fear of heights was ... but instead of commenting on it, she went over and kissed him on the cheek.

"Are you sure you don't want me to stay down there with you? I don't mind, really."

"That's a firm no," David said, winking at her. "After spending so much time with you under the same roof, I'm in serious need of some peace and quiet."

She laughed, kissed him again, this time on the mouth, and then backed away from him.

"I might just swing by once or twice to see how you're doing."

"Peace and quiet," he repeated, firing an invisible bullet at her with a thumb and forefinger gun. "You can wave. I'll allow that, but nothing more."

With those words, he turned on his heels and walked down the ramp, while the other three continued all the way up to the top.

chapter 22

The view from the platform certainly wasn't bad, but it was probably a good decision David had made to stay down below. Because it was pretty high up, and since the railing along the edge consisted of thin metal pipes with no plates in between, it was almost impossible not to look down.

On the positive side, the open design of the railing allowed Billy to see what was going on in the field, even though he was sitting in the wheelchair.

So far, though, it had been more interesting to look up than down, as nothing new happened on the field. It was still just the same, constantly-increasing flock of people drawing in on the stage like metal shavings to a magnet.

The sky above them, on the other hand, had plenty of drama and excitement to offer, as the dark gray clouds from earlier had now gotten company. They were pulling a tail of other clouds behind them, some almost completely black, thereby forming an oblong figure in the shape of a gala dress.

Before long, that dress's dark skirt would sway in over Redwater football stadium's open roof—perhaps bringing a storm.

As if she had read this thought in Randall's head, Rose leaned against the railing next to him and said:

"Who would have thought we'd miss the weather forecasts?"

"Not me," Randall said. "I was the first to complain when they got it wrong."

Rose nodded, and something changed in her eyes. If Randall had to guess, he'd say it was a memory from life before the Collapse that popped up and gave her a sting of sorrow. It was something he knew only too well.

"How long do you think it'll be before they're ready?" she asked.

"Not long," he said, pointing down at one of the

arched passages on the other side. "They're closing the entrance over there."

Rose tilted her head back and sighed heavily. Then she squatted next to Billy and put her elbow on the wheelchair's armrest.

"I'm bored, Billy. Aren't you?"

Billy shook his head and patted her on the arm. And then, with a pronunciation that was clearer than it had been at any point since they brought him out of the hospital in Newcrest, he said:

"Fun, Rose. Just you wait."

For a moment, Rose looked completely stunned. Then she smiled and poked lovingly at Billy's shoulder.

"Well, we're full of surprises today, aren't we?"

Behind them, somewhere down on the field, sounded a loud, creaky click, followed by a man's voice amplified by a megaphone—and so distorted that it took some time for Randall to realize that he knew its owner.

"On behalf of the Redwater camp, I would like to welcome you all," Whitmoore said. "We are very humbled with the large turnout ... but then again, who wouldn't want to take part on a day like this?"

He hesitated and uttered a dry, gurgling laugh.

"I was about to say on a day like this when the light finally returns after a long period of darkness," he said, pointing up to the dark clouds in the sky. "But, well, as you can see ..."

He's a natural, Randall thought, when he saw the entire assembly on the field looking upward on Whitmoore's command—to then erupt in subdued but warm laughter.

"But while we may not get to see the light today, there's no reason to be sad," Whitmoore continued. "Because when I look around from up here, I see more than just the faces of old—and hopefully lots of new—friends. I see something that for too long has been in short supply. I see *hope*!"

Another well-chosen break, so the crowd's enthusiastic response was allowed to resound, and then Whitmoore calmed them down again by clearing his throat.

"Hope is a good start, but of course it isn't enough in itself. Achieving the dream of rebuilding our society and getting our lives back requires more. It requires will, cooperation, trust, and humanity."

"Was he a preacher or something?" Rose whispered, while Whitmoore paused for another short moment. "Before the Collapse, I mean."

Randall shrugged.

"Maybe. He's very eloquent. Definitely trained in talking to large crowds ... but I always figured he was military or something like that."

"But before we start with all the big plans for the future," Whitmoore continued. "Let me make one thing clear right away: we are gathered here to look to the future. But looking to the future doesn't mean that we shouldn't be allowed to look to the past. Because everyone here is in the same boat. Everyone has lost someone close to them. Everyone is a survivor—and not necessarily by choice. And for some, the idea of rebuilding a normal life—of having to *live* again—might trigger some kind of shame or guilt toward the ones they cared about who didn't get the same chance. But to that ..."

He said something more, but by then Randall had stopped listening. Because there was something down at the edge of the field just below them that had caught his attention.

It couldn't be ... could it?

Now it was back, and this time he saw it clearly: a light blue, open-faced denim vest over a black T-shirt with Metallica's logo printed under a metal skull with flames in the eye sockets.

"Rose, I need you to keep an eye on Billy for a minute," he said, and without waiting for her answer, he started running toward the ramp. "I'll be right back. I promise."

"But, but ... where are you going?"

"It's Tommy. He's down there."

chapter 23

In his confusion—and in his eagerness to reach his brother before he disappeared once more into the crowd—Randall didn't have time to consider how he actually felt about Tommy right now.

Was he angry? Was what happened with the bag and the drugs really *unforgivable*, as he had said when the argument was at its peak?

Or was he really just relieved that his brother was back and that he was unharmed? Maybe he was even happy to see him *here* of all places. Because wasn't it a sign of good faith that Tommy showed up here and participated in something he really didn't believe in, but which Randall had tried to convince him was a good idea?

All these questions whirled around in Randall's head as he ran down the ramp. But when he paused at the foot of it and got another glimpse of his brother out there on the overgrown field, everything fell into place by itself.

The anger was still there, in the background, of course it was. But it was worry that had been the dominant feeling in his heart, and it was *relief* that took its place now.

"Randall? What's going on?" he heard a voice saying behind him.

It was David. Out of the corner of his eyes Randall had seen him sitting on the ground with his back against one of the concrete pillars that kept the disabled platform afloat ... but he didn't have time to stop and explain. He had to talk to Tommy before he disappeared out of sight again.

He ran down the concrete stairway and then a few feet out onto the field, where he stopped again.

And there, both standing with their feet buried in a weathered, yellowish sea of grass under a dark sky, which had now started to cry, the two brothers made eye contact.

Tommy saw him, he saw Tommy, and for a moment looking at him was like standing in front of a mirror reflecting the relief he felt himself.

But then Tommy looked past him and upwards, and something suddenly changed in his gray eyes. The relief transformed into shock and horror.

The next second, Tommy's gaze moved downward in one quick jolt, and although Randall himself didn't have time to turn around, the sounds he heard behind him drew a frighteningly clear picture.

There were three sounds; a surprised scream, followed by a hard bump, and finally a crunchy sound, like when breaking a bundle of celery in two.

He turned around ... and stiffened.

Rose was lying on the wide concrete staircase he himself had just been on. She lay on her back with her arms hanging limply to the sides and her upper body facing the sky as if she were welcoming the increasing rain.

Except that she didn't have her eyes on the sky, for the collision with the hard concrete of the stairs had broken her neck, so her head now hung down over the edge of one of the steps, forced backward at an unnatural angle.

Behind Randall, the buzzing of the crowd and Whitmoore's distorted voice faded out as they too realized what had happened.

Inside himself something similar occurred. Everything faded out and went quiet. His thoughts crumbled, and any attempt to pull meaning out of what he was staring at, his brain answered with empty silence.

Even when he saw David—deadly pale and with a deranged expression in his eyes—come crashing down the stairs in the direction of his lifeless girlfriend, he was unable to move.

It wasn't until he heard the familiar high-pitched tones of Billy's panic bell that he gained the strength to force his gaze away from Rose and David.

He let it slide up in a straight line until it met Billy. He stood by the platform railing, ringing the bell up against the dark gray sky as if he were trying to awaken some drowsy god.

Wait.

He was *standing* up there. *Upright*.

No, his brain had to be playing tricks on him. It was the only plausible explanation. The shock of seeing Rose lying there on the stairs must have made him hallucinate.

Possibly—but no matter how many times he blinked, Billy still stood up on the platform, swinging the damned bell back and forth, producing a steady stream of high-pitched, metallic tones that resonated in the arena. What the hell was he doing?

A terrible foreboding struck Randall, and the second after, it was confirmed.

Behind Billy, way up on the top edge of the oval building, a misty silhouette appeared. Then one more ... and one more.

Slowly, they toned in; gray figures, gradually taking human shape, while slowly forming a ring that ran almost all the way around the upper edge of the arena.

"It looks like ... children?" Randall heard a voice say somewhere behind him, and he knew right away that it was true. That the small gray figures up there didn't just *look like* kids.

They *were* kids. The kids from the hospitals.

Children who—like Billy—had had a silvery liquid filled with small, alien creatures pumped into their veins.

Billy hadn't tried to wake up a drowsy god with his bell ... but he *had* called for something. He had given a signal.

As an unpleasant extension of that thought, he now saw Billy reach his arm out over the platform railing and let go of the bell. It landed on the stairs five feet from where David sat with Rose in his arms, sobbing.

Still paralyzed by the shock, Randall could do nothing but watch helplessly as his son held his arm outstretched above the railing for a moment, after which he lifted it up to the sky and clenched his hand.

Behind him—and all around the top edge of the stadium—the children mirrored this movement.

Except Billy had let go of what he had in his hand while they maintained their grip on what could only be the service guns of the departed police force.

Now they stood there, an army of children, with

their weapons ready, obviously waiting for their leader's signal.

"RANDALL! IT'S AN AMBUSH! WE'VE GOT TO GET OUT, NOW! GET DAVID AWAY FROM THERE!"

Tommy's warning reached his ears, and Randall started to turn around, but he could only do it slowly—*far too* slowly—as his body felt as if it were submerged in thick mud up to his chest.

"RANDALL, IT'S—

That was as far as Tommy got before Billy slammed his hand with the invisible judge's hammer down in one quick jolt.

The first bullet came alone, and for a few seconds Randall thought it was just the bang from it being fired that had drowned out Tommy's voice.

But then he saw Tommy's hands move up to his neck, grab it—and then get painted dark red.

Above them, in an eerily stark contrast, Tommy's pale face pulled together in shock and pain, while his eyes—foggy and blinking rapidly—asked Randall what had happened.

And then, without grace and on a rain-soaked

deathbed of weathered, yellowish grass that wasn't worthy of him, Tommy Morgan fell down and closed his eyes for the last time.

chapter 24

Get off your ass, Randall, ordered the thought version of Allie in the back of his head, but her order was only one of many thoughts mercilessly being swirled and thrown around by the waves in the rough sea that was Randall's mind.

On the field, chaos reigned as well. The crowd—the invited guests on this day of hope—stumbled around, bumped into each other, slipped on the grass, tripped over each other, *pushed* each other, jumped and crawled. All to avoid the bullets that hailed down on them from above.

He should be doing the same. Running, screaming, pushing, and crawling in a panic. But he was still paralyzed, and all he could do was stare alternately back and forth between Tommy's lifeless body and Billy up on the platform.

Somewhere on the edge of his consciousness, he was aware that these two things were intertwined. For some reason, his brain just couldn't—or wouldn't—clarify the connection for him right now.

Somewhere to his left sounded a loud, despairing scream. When he looked over there, he saw a woman standing with one hand locked around the wrist of her other arm—which now only had a macabre red fountain in the place where her hand should have been.

He didn't recognize her right away. It wasn't until she raised her head and made eye contact with him that he realized it was Mary, Rose's neighbor.

Her eyes asked him—*begged* him—for help, but all Randall could sense to do was point over at Tommy's lifeless body and exclaim:

"They're ... *stepping* on him, Mary. They keep stepping on him."

Part of him could hear what an absurd thing it was to say in the situation, and part of him understood it was the shock that spoke.

But part of him was genuinely confused—insulted, even—at how disrespectfully they just trampled over his brother. After all, they were survivors, too, weren't they? They should know better. Had they not had family themselves, so they ...

Family. Oh God, David.

He turned around and spotted David, who was still sitting on the stairs holding Rose in his arms. Above them hovered a grayish mist, which had to be gun smoke from the children's guns.

The sight of the smoke alerted Randall to the smell. The lead-heavy, suffocating stench of burnt gunpowder that stuck in his throat and threatened to close his windpipe. The smell of Fourth of July, the smell of New Year's Eve ... and now forever the smell of the worst moment of his life.

A hard blow to his shoulder caused him to wobble sideways. He turned around and saw the culprit—a man with a large, bleeding hole where one eye should have been—sprinting across the grass and then diving in between the plastic seats in the front row.

Some distance behind him was another man lying on the grass. He had also been shot in the face. Had it not been for the clothes and the bald head, where only a small cluster of cork brown hair was rooted, Randall wouldn't have been able to tell that it was the Mayor.

From the Mayor's lifeless body, his gaze slipped back to David on the stairs, and in that very instant, Allie's voice sent a deeply disturbing thought through his head:

If you don't get him out of there, he's going to end up the same.

He tried to do what Allie commanded, tried to shout David's name, but what came out was nothing but a suffocated hiss.

Drenched in panic, he ran instead, stumbling, like all the other desperate people behind him who tumbled aimlessly around on the football field, trampling across more and more of their fallen comrades.

Except Randall didn't tumble around aimlessly. He *had* a goal: he needed to rescue the young Romeo, who sat on the stairs clutching his lifeless Juliet, apparently without even noticing the completely insane scenario playing out around him.

"David!" he tried again, and this time the name

came out. "David, I need you to come with me!"

The sound of his own name made David look up, but he didn't make any attempt to stand up. He simply looked blankly at Randall, who had now reached the stairs.

"David, you have to—"

A sound—a fast flick, like when an insect whizzes quickly past one's ear at high speed—cut through the constant bangs from the guns for some reason and hit Randall's ear canal loud and clear; almost as if his brain had focused solely on it.

With the sound came a blistering sting in his thigh, and for a split second he thought that he might actually have been stung by an insect.

But looking down at his leg, discovering the round hole in his jeans and watching the fabric turn purple around it, he realized what the real explanation was.

Ignore it. Ignore it and keep going!

He looked up, tried to focus on David, but the smoke had gotten denser. It burned in his eyes, blurred his eyesight, and caused his gaze to slide upwards, so that instead of finding David and Rose on the stairs, it ended up on the platform.

On Billy. His son, the traitor. The enemy's secret weapon. The real ...

No, you're confused, in shock. It's the pain, the bullet in your thigh, making you talk nonsense!

But no, it wasn't nonsense, and although the pain in the thigh was severe, it was nothing compared to that realization.

Because he understood it now. He saw the truth, and he saw the monster. Saw it standing up there on the platform with a hateful smile on its lips as it commanded its murderous army of children around with his son's small, pale hands. Led them like an orchestral leader with an invisible baton.

And as he stood there, staring at his son, a slew of fragmented memories, together forming a gruesome motif, started to wash over Randall. Small waves quickly turning into a devastating tsunami.

He saw himself standing down by the mass grave in the riverbed with Billy's cap in his hand, staring up the slope, deeply puzzled by how it could have ended up so far down if it had not been thrown.

He saw Martha Hymnwell, heard her ask if it was Billy they were looking for and then telling them she had seen his wheelchair sitting empty down by the Radio House.

He heard Rose's now-handless neighbor saying that Billy had run off once while she was looking after him, but that it was probably just to get a break from her stories and that she had found him outside the medicine storage.

And he saw ... oh God, the bag of drugs that he had found in Tommy's backpack *after* Billy had been alone with it. The bag which, unsurprisingly, had caused him to rush into the living room to scold Tommy while Billy stayed alone out in the workshop ... with the radio.

This last realization was too much for Randall. Way too much. He staggered sideways, tried to grab ahold of one of the outer seats, but misjudged the distance and tumbled in over it instead.

The hard plastic backrest hit him in the side, just below the ribs, and pushed the air out of him, causing a flurry of small, silvery spots to pop out all over his field of view.

Something grabbed him, *pulled* him. He instinctively tried to resist and pull free, but it didn't work. The person pulling him simply grabbed harder—and where before there had only been one hand pulling at his upper arm, Randall now felt two arms cross in over his chest, where they locked themselves together.

"Let me go," he snarled as the pull came and he was dragged further along the floor between the rows of seats. "You won't—"

"Randall, it's me," sounded right next to his ear. "Stop fighting."

"D-David?"

"Yeah, it's me."

"Oh, my God, David. It was Billy, h-he ... and your Rose, she ... oh no, David, I ..."

"Be quiet," David replied in a voice that was more cynical and commanding than Randall had ever heard it. It sounded like David wouldn't hesitate to move his arms from his rib cage up to his neck if the subject wasn't dropped immediately. "We have to get out now, and our only chance is to stay in hiding down here between the seats. Can you crawl?"

Randall moved his hand down to his thigh and gently pressed around the wound. It was bleeding and it hurt, but it wasn't unbearable.

"I think so."

"Good, then follow me."

Randall did what he was told and began pulling himself forward on the cold concrete floor between the seats. Every once in a while, he bumped his leg against one of the metal bars under the seats, triggering a cascade of white-hot pain in his thigh.

But he swallowed it, kept his eyes focused on the soles of David's shoes, and did his best to keep up as he pulled himself across the floor, using only his hands.

When they made it to the next stairway at the end of the rows of seats, David paused and raised his hand to catch Randall's attention—and when he had it, he pointed to something over in the next section of stands.

"Do you see it?"

Randall squinted but found that the only thing he could identify in the dense smoke was another inhumane obstacle course filled with plastic seats.

"See what?"

"The emergency exit. The door."

It took a moment, but then he managed to spot it. A little farther up, maybe three rows of chairs above their own level, a hexagonal, bunker-like structure stuck up amidst all the plastic seats. And in the center of it was a door that, as David had pointed out, was marked:

EMERGENCY EXIT.

"And what do we do if it's ..."

Locked would have been the last word in that sentence if Randall hadn't realized that this hardly would be the case, since emergency exits by definition were designed to be opened from the inside, whether locked or not.

"Never mind," he said, shaking his head. "How do we get over there?"

David didn't answer. Instead, he carefully got up on one knee and looked out between two of the chairs ... but he only stayed up there for a few seconds before he pulled away again and lay down. Made himself small.

"What it is? What did you see?"

"It's the kids," David whispered in a voice that was no longer cynical and cold, but instead testified that the limit of what his psyche could handle had almost been reached. "They're heading down the stairs now, and they're ... fuck, Randall, their eyes. They're *cold. Ice cold.*"

Hearing David lose control hurt Randall, but at the same time it forced him to find and tap into a reserve stockpile of his own strength.

"Breathe," he said. "Deep breaths, slowly, one by one. Try to ignore the noise."

Noise? That's a pretty mild term for the sound of a mass execution, don't you think?

In a way, she was right. It was a mild term for the gunfire, the screams, and all the other terrible noises that surrounded them. But Randall had neither the time nor the energy to have a semantic discussion with the snide thought-version of his ex-wife, and therefore he followed his own advice and threw Allie's voice into the same category. *Noise.*

"Just close your eyes and fill your lungs. That's it. Better?"

David nodded.

"Good. The kids were going down the stairs, you said. Was it all of them?"

David nodded again.

"So, when they've passed by us, they'll have their backs turned, right?"

Now David opened his eyes. He then nodded for the third time.

"Okay," Randall said. "Then that's our chance. We'll hide here and wait. Once they're past us, we'll cross the stairs. Deal?"

"Deal."

With that word, a plan was made, and both Randall and David rolled as far in under the faded blue plastic seats as they could.

Then they waited, both with their eyes fixated on the many shoes, moving step by step down the stairs a little farther up.

There was, however, one pair of sneakers that stood out among the rest and made Randall turn his eyes away for a bit. He saw David do the same.

The sneakers were a pair of white Nikes with pink laces. The socks in them were also white ...

and at the top of them, just below the edge of the pants, the logo could be glimpsed.

Hello Kitty.

chapter 25

The wait was excruciating. One thing was that they were lying there, unable to do anything but listen as the children made their way downward while continuing to shoot at the remaining survivors on the field. Another thing was that Randall's blood loss could really be felt when he was lying still, and it became increasingly difficult for him to stay conscious.

"Don't close your eyes," whispered David, who had also noticed the problem. "There's only two more left, and then the coast is clear."

Randall nodded and shook his head.

It didn't help much. The black veil on the edge of his field of vision lingered ... but he was awake enough to focus on the two pairs of shoes that David was talking about. They were passing them now, and they indeed appeared to be the last ones.

Now David raised his hand, first with five fingers outstretched, then with four ... three ... two ... one.

They started crawling, David in front, Randall right behind. The first part of the way, where they had to climb up and across the stairs to reach the right level, they moved slowly and constantly with an eye on the children farther down. Once they had gotten to the other side, though, they picked up the pace, and Randall returned to his previous strategy of fixating his eyes on the soles of David's shoes.

Like most emergency exits, the door was equipped with a long handle that went across it and ensured that the door could be opened from the inside without the need for a key.

Since David got there first, he was the one who sat up, grabbed the handle, and pulled it down. He did it with quivering hands and so slowly that Randall for a moment thought the door actually *was* locked after all.

But then came the click. The door slipped open, and what they found behind it was a long, narrow hallway, leading directly out to the parking lot.

"Hey, are you coming?" David whispered, after which, without waiting for an answer, he crawled as far into the hallway as he could without letting go of the door.

Randall hesitated, bit his lip, and then glanced back in the direction of the platform. He could see neither it nor Billy because of the smoke.

"Later," David said solemnly, reaching out his hand. "I promise."

After another moment of hesitation—and another few futile glances back—Randall accepted his hand and let himself be dragged into the narrow hallway.

THREE MONTHS LATER

— EPILOGUE —

It's the sound of the motorcycle in the distance that pulls him out of the emotional moment and makes him take the bag of silvery liquid out of the light and put it into the darkness of his inner pocket instead.

He then wipes the tears off his cheeks and starts walking back through the aisle of the semi-dark auditorium.

He's not in a hurry. Judging by the sound, the motorcycle is still some way from the hospital. Of course, it can be misleading when there are walls in between, but in general all sounds are surprisingly clear in cities as deserted and abandoned as Newcrest. Besides, the snow and icy roads will also force David to drive slowly.

From the auditorium he proceeds directly toward the door to the staircase that led him up here, but something causes him to hesitate and remove his hand from the handle again as soon as he has put it there.

It's a memory from his first visit to this place.

Another memory.

He turns away from the door and starts to walk along the corridor until he gets to an intersection where the central hallway is connected to two adjacent hallways.

Although only the first twelve to fifteen yards of the aisle on the left side can be seen before it ends in a closed double door, this is the one Randall enters without hesitation. Because he knows what's behind those doors.

As he pushes them open, he feels a drag wind whizzing by. Like a ghost of the past, it caresses his cheeks with icy fingers, after which it disappears into the hallway behind him.

It isn't difficult to see where the ghost came in, because near the middle of the walkway in which he now stands, there lies a pile of snow on the floor. Above it is a broken window—perhaps vandalism, perhaps just a result of the passage of time.

The walkway is a link between two of the hospital's buildings, free-floating at the height of the fourth floor, and Randall vividly recalls how he had to distract David while crossing it so his fear of heights wouldn't take over.

Once over on the other side, Randall takes a moment to look around. He knows the stairwell is nearby, but he just can't remember where—and the last time he had an illuminated sign to navigate by.

Just as he's about to give up, he spots a hospital bed that someone has left in the middle of the hallway. He knows he's passed that bed before, because he remembers the sheet hanging loosely down, one corner twisted into one of the bed's wheels. It's still jammed in there.

He walks down the hallway, passing the bed as well as some coffee tables, and then he spots the neon sign with the green man and the green door, neither of which will probably ever light up again.

If he wanted to, he could take the stairs all the way down to the bottom floor, but it's the door to the main hallway on the first floor that he opens. There's something at the end of that hallway he wants to see before he leaves the hospital.

Why he's drawn to that section, though, he doesn't quite know. Last time it was an extremely unpleasant experience to step in there, and there is no reason to think it will be better this time around.

But still, he continues through the corridor until the double door appears. The one carrying the text:

B7: PEDIATRIC WARD / BED SECTION.

When he pushes this door open, he's prepared. He knows exactly what's waiting on the other side. Nevertheless, he must swallow a lump at the sight of the empty beds, where the duvets and sheets hang crookedly down over the edges, as if the patients tried to cling to them while they were being pulled out against their will.

His gaze slips to the left, and suddenly it's perfectly clear to him why his subconscious mind insisted on sending him in here.

The drawing of the bumblebee is still there. One among many other children's drawings hanging on the bulletin board next to the toy rack.

He reaches out his hand, strokes two fingers gently along the edge of the bumblebee's all-too-small wings, and then across the artist's signature down in the corner.

He wonders if *MARCUS 7 YEARS* could still be alive. If he could be out there somewhere.

Probably not. Why should this young artist have had more luck than all the other children?

Or less luck.

He pulls the drawing down, folds it, and puts it in the back pocket of his jeans. He then leaves Ward B7 and starts walking back through the main corridor toward the hospital entrance.

Almost at the exact moment when he puts his foot on the first step of the broken escalator leading down to the entrance hall, Randall hears the motorcycle arriving—and then getting turned off—just outside.

Halfway down the stairs, he can also see it through the entrance hall windows. It's parked behind his own car. A little farther ahead is David. He is wrapped in a thick winter coat with a hood, the fur edge of which is filled with small, hard clumps of snow.

Under the hood is David's face. It's no longer a young man's face. It hasn't been since Redwater.

Since Rose.

The eyes show it most clearly. Those eyes—which are currently studying the wreckage of Tommy's old Chevrolet—have been devoid of joy ever since.

Even when David's lips pull up in a rare smile, his eyes never follow.

He'd probably say the same about you, Randall. Don't you think?

"Isn't it hard to stay warm on that thing?" Randall shouts as he steps off the escalator.

David glances back at the motorcycle and then shakes his head, causing some of the snow nuggets to sprinkle off his hood.

"I'll survive," he says. "How'd it go? Did you find it?"

Randall opens his jacket so David can see the bag sticking out of its inside pocket.

"I was right. It was on the floor, below the seat."

"Can I see it?"

Randall hesitates, doesn't quite know why, but then takes the bag out of his pocket and hands it over to David, as they meet by a broken window in the facade.

David turns the bag in his hands and then holds it up against the backlight from the sky to study it closer. Meanwhile, Randall pulls off his thick scarf again and wraps it around his hand so he doesn't cut himself on the sill as he jumps through the broken window.

"Gross," David mutters, giving back the bag.

Randall shrugs and then starts walking toward the car. However, he stops when he discovers that David hasn't moved.

"Is something wrong?"

"It's just ... I actually managed to get a lead today. A *real* lead."

"Oh yeah?"

"I came across a small group of survivors from somewhere near Williamsport. They were on the run because their camp was attacked the day before yesterday. By a group of kids. Chances are it's them, but ... well, now you've found the bag."

For a while, those words are allowed to hang in the air, while David shrugs and rubs his hands together to warm them.

"Was there a question hidden in there, David?" Randall asks, though he knows full well what his traveling companion wants to know.

"Knowing that... are we still sticking to the plan? I guess that's what I'm asking."

To his own surprise, Randall hesitates before answering. Perhaps because he at this very moment realizes that he is carrying the almost perfect symbolic depiction of the crossroads he's standing at in the two back pockets of his jeans. The child's drawing of a bumblebee in the right back pocket, the business card from the ARL Research Facility in the left. A coincidence so unlikely that it could have been something he had devised for one of his own books.

"Yeah," he finally says, after which he turns around again and starts walking toward the car. "We stick to the plan."

THIS IS NOT

-THE END-

— THANK YOU TO —

Sarah Jacobsen, who is my eternal first reader and my sworn accomplice in this life. She's the one with whom I take all the big leaps. And if the height makes me doubt, she never hesitates to give me a loving push.

Kaare & Karina Bertelsen Dantoft, who once again have accepted the roles of beta readers. For that, as well as our friendship, I am deeply grateful.

Lastly—but by no means least—I owe a huge thank you to you, **dear reader**. Our time is precious, and as always, I thank you for yours.

— Per Jacobsen

Made in the USA
Monee, IL
03 April 2024

56304011R00177